The Price of Ki[illegible]

By Richard Masters

A compelling tale of good and evil, as experienced by two young children, scarred by a life of abuse and neglect.

Richard Masters was born in London. He was educated in Woking and at the University of London, Goldsmiths College, where he qualified as a teacher. In his late teens he spent two years working in a remote area of New Guinea; the subject of his book 'The Sago Swamp'. In 1974 he started his teaching career in Southeast London and, in 1985, moved to Somerset. He has also worked as an estate manager, an actor, an extra in many TV series and a part-time university lecturer at Bath Spa University. He has previously written plays for stage, scripts for a touring theatre group and many articles for Times Educational Supplement and others. He remains in Somerset with his wife, Susan, and dog, Arthur.

<u>Previous books</u>

As it should Be	A political fantasy
The Sago Swamp	A Story of Joy, Despair and Adventure deep in the Interior of New Guinea

Both are available on Amazon.

'There is a moment every night when the sunbeams disappear and the moonbeams peep out across the countryside, turning the velvet black of the forest, into a beautiful picture of gold, amber and green.'

Barry remembered hearing, or maybe reading those words somewhere in the past and, whenever he thought of them, he couldn't help but smile.

He wasn't smiling now. The forest looked cold and dark, a place of fear and evil.

A place in which his friend was taking her last walk in this world.

A walk that would end in her death.

Chapter 1 Two Sides of the Coin

Justin McBride was fully aware of his reputation as a vicious, sadistic man who took a perverse pleasure in inflicting pain and suffering. He not only embraced it but considered it part of his make-up. Yet, even in his brutality, a genuine sense of satisfaction eluded him. His actions stemmed from, what in his mind, was a necessity. He did it because, in his world, he had to dominate and control every person or situation he met. The more he was feared, the more the world, as he saw it, would bend to his will.

His life was devoid of friendship or any real relationships. He was married, but he hated his wife and two children. The girl had some uses, but the boy was always hanging around him like a dog wanting to be petted.

In the early years of his marriage, he had tried to love his wife but he found he was incapable of love or anything remotely close to it. Everything she did filled him with rage. So, he beat her, until her spirit was broken and she was totally compliant. The only thing he left her with was her addiction to alcohol.

Or so he thought, but then he discovered her treachery. He found that she was planning to sneak away and take the two brats with her. She had phoned her aunt and asked if she could stay with her for a while. Her aunt: her stupid, old, sore ridden, ugly, monstrosity of an aunt.

He had made it clear to her, early in their marriage, that she was never again to contact her family or her friends from her old life and she had disobeyed him, gone behind his back. And now, she was going to pay the price.

Daniel Pitt was the fourth and last child of Tess and Charles Pitt. The age gap between himself and his next brother was seven years. The truth is, he was an accident.

His mother died of a heart attack when he was thirteen. His dad, who was working twelve hours a day in his failing electrical business, did not have the capacity or the energy to give Daniel the help he needed. His brothers had all left home and, as he went to school miles away, he had no close friends. He found himself struggling through his days without really taking in what was happening around him. He felt lost and could not break away from the feeling of always being sad and afraid.

Then one day his form teacher, Miss Sinclair, asked him to stay after registration. She said she had noticed that he looked as if something was wrong and wondered if he wanted to tell her anything. He burst into tears, the first time he had cried since his mother's funeral. Miss Sinclair took him in her arms and held him. She waited patiently for him to tell her what the problem was.

"My mum died; she had cancer."

"I'm so sorry. I didn't know." She said.

Miss Sinclair invited Daniel to come and see her in her office any lunchtime he wished and when he did, she held his hand and gently encouraged him to talk. Slowly, over the following weeks, he found an outlet for his grief and his recovery began.

Daniel had very few other memories from the early part of his life. He remembered that in primary school he had shown some creativity in his weekly drama lessons; his teacher encouraged him to make up and write short plays for the class to perform. But that had been knocked out of him once he moved up to secondary. Apart from that, he was not particularly good at anything, academic work, crafts or sport.

His O'level exams were about to start in about a month, when at the end of one of his maths lessons his teacher, Mr Saunders, kept him back.

"Pitt, you are not really expected to pass any of your O'levels, but I think you could scrape through maths if you really tried. But you've got to work hard and revise thoroughly. Look, I'm always here after school for an hour. If you're having a problem or want some help, come and see me."

Daniel did go to see him, several times, but the fact Mr Saunders was willing to take the trouble to do that made a difference to all his subjects. He ended up scraping a pass in all nine, much to the amazement of everyone. His dad was as proud as punch and Mr Saunders bought him a huge bar of chocolate.

The kindness shown by both Miss Sinclair and Mr Saunders had a profound effect on Daniel and moulded the way he was to become, as a father, a teacher and as a person. He always tried to see the best in people and draw that out.

Years later, when being interviewed for a job at Wells Community School he was asked how he dealt with naughty and disruptive pupils. He said.

"Find and nurture the good and, eventually, the bad will melt away."

He lived his life by that mantra, although, his children got thoroughly fed up with him reeling it off every time they were naughty.

At the age of twenty, he moved to London and trained to be a teacher at Goldsmiths College in New Cross, with mathematics and later drama as his main subjects. It was tough, but with the help of some brilliant teachers, he gained his degree. In his summer holidays he worked for a travelling theatre group as an actor and writer.

After leaving college, he started his teaching career in a seriously difficult school in southeast London. The staff who worked there were a diverse group of men and women. Some were inept and lazy but others were brilliant, taking the many teenagers who were neglected, angry and violent and showing them a world where they could find respect, kindness and success.

After eleven years, Daniel, with his wife and young family, moved to the Mendip Hills in Somerset. He had been selected to head the maths department in a school in Wells.

In his third year in Somerset, tragedy befell the Pitt family. His wife Mary was diagnosed with a cancerous tumour in the brain, and after two dreadful months of pain and anguish for her and the whole family, she died.

Daniel took a month off work so he could always be there for his young family whenever they needed him.

He remained at the school for the rest of his career and at the age of fifty five he retired, and, with his children all having moved away, he took up writing. He wrote three books that sadly and spectacularly failed to persuade any agent or publisher to see the excellence of his work; so obvious to him, but sadly, not to anyone else.

When he had first met Mary and had fallen in love, he not only gained a wife but also an Irish setter as well. There had been an Irish setter in his life ever since.

Chapter 2 The Rescue

Sunshine Mawa had been a professional boxer from the age of twenty. Now at nearly forty, he knew he was pretty much finished. He was unfit, vastly overweight and no longer had the willpower to do anything about it.

There had been times in his career when he had done well, beating some good fighters and earnt a lot of respect and money, but he'd never quite made it to the top. Maybe he could have done if he'd shown a greater commitment and listened to his coach a bit more. But now, having fritted away his earnings on women, drink and drugs, he was flat broke.

He sometimes thought back to the day John Malinga had plucked him from the streets of Peckham, where he lived in a slum tenement, with his mum and dad and five brothers and sisters. His parents had done their best, but, like every other kid on the estate, he mixed with the wrong crowd and occasionally got himself into minor trouble with the police. Malinga was running a local scheme to take teenagers off the streets and introduce them to the discipline, comradery and confidence that boxing could give. He had seen potential in Sunshine and become his lifelong coach and friend. But try as he might he had failed to persuade him that to get to the very top he had to forsake the joys of, rum, hash and late nights of debauchery. How he wished he'd listened.

So, when, in the early hours of the morning, as he was leaving the Bright Moon Club in New Cross, two men, he had never seen before, approached him and offered him a job, which he accepted without having to think very hard. They explained what was expected of him and told him he would be paid five hundred pounds for ten minutes work; that was a decent payday.

Apparently some guy was going to give him a beating, that was all. He chuckled to himself; he'd had plenty of beatings in his career and maybe he'd throw a few punches back, just to make it a look bit more authentic. He wondered what it was all about. Perhaps the guy was showing off to his girlfriend or wanted to warn somebody who was upsetting him. Anyway, it didn't really matter to him, five hundred pounds was five hundred pounds, and would keep him in food, drink and drugs for a week, maybe longer if he was careful. That was all that mattered.

As often happened, that night he couldn't sleep, his mind started churning over the mistakes he'd made and the wrong decisions he'd taken. As much as he tried to stave off these thoughts, they refused to go, sucking at his fragile self-esteem and trivialising his life. He could do nothing to fight off the feeling of utter helplessness and failure.

There had been a time when he wouldn't even consider working for five hundred pounds; he had been guaranteed thousands every fight, win or lose. Sadly, those days were long gone.

The guys offering him the job were obviously muscle, working for someone important, perhaps a gang leader or bent coppers. They had made it clear, that if he ever thought about telling the police it was a setup, he and his sister's family would suffer the consequences. He could tell they were serious. He wondered how they knew about her; they must have done their research. They needn't have said it though, he wasn't a grass. Maybe though, sometime in the future, he might go back and ask for a bit more money. Perhaps when he was desperate and really needed it.

A thought struck him. Perhaps he could persuade them to offer him a job, he knew he could be a real asset; bouncer or bodyguard, not an enforcer though, he didn't fancy that too much. Despite being a boxer, he wasn't really a naturally violent man.

Barry Payne got out of the car and shivered as the cold late evening breeze enveloped him. He watched as Don Fenton and George Pamment walked to the rear and opened the boot. Despite the evening turning dark, he could still just make out the figure of Kim McBride as they hauled her out. They left her hands tied behind her back but ripped off the tape covering her mouth.

"Hello darling," smirked Fenton, "fancy a walk in the woods, see a bit of wildlife?"

They were parked at the end of a track leading from Hosey Common Road, just off the M25 near Westerham. A narrow footpath led into the forest. During the day, this place would be a popular destination for dog walkers and joggers, but now it was deserted and eerily silent. As they dragged her down the path she turned her head and looked towards Barry.

"Please Barry, help me."

Barry turned away, he couldn't bear to meet her pleading eyes,

"Barry, please."

As they seemed to melt into the gloom of the forest, Barry stood still, tears welling up. For a minute or so more, he could hear Kim begging for help, but then all went silent, all that was left was the soft moan of the breeze rustling the leaves in the trees and an owl hooting mournfully in the distance.

He got back in the car and looked at the clock, nine thirty. He started the engine, turned the heating on as high as it would go and put the radio on. Gerry and the Pacemakers' 'You'll never walk alone' was playing, it was one of his favourite songs. It gave him no joy tonight though; Kim was his friend; they were killing her and he was doing nothing to stop them. He put his head in his hands and wept.

At about the same time, Justin McBride was standing at the bar of the Golden Lion pub in Penge. He'd never been there before and he liked it. It was old fashioned, no youngsters congregating around a jukebox or playing on the pool table, a real local for serious drinkers.

The door opened and Sunshine Mawa sauntered in and looked around. He wondered if they'd throw him out, the clientele was exclusively white. He swaggered up to the bar and ordered a rum and coke. There was no problem however and the attractive young bar maid was happy to serve him.

"I needs a piss darlin," he said to her with a wink, "where's the lav love? See what I done there, a bi of poery."

She pointed to the other end of the room without comment. He followed her direction, and as he weaved past McBride, he lurched into him, knocking his pint glass of beer so that it spilt down his shirt. He laughed.

"Sorry mate. I's a bit unsteady on mar feet," he said, although he didn't sound as though he was terribly sorry.

McBride just glared at him and then, without any warning, he brought his knee up, hard into Sunshine's groin. Sunshine was taken completely by surprise and bent over forwards; he was in agony. McBride grabbed his dreadlocks and pulled him upright before head butting him full in the face. The noise of Sunshine's nose breaking could clearly be heard throughout the pub. He fell to the ground moaning with pain, and for the next few minutes McBride kicked and punched him in a sustained attack that looked as if it could only end with the victim's death. The punters at the Golden Lion had seen a few fights in the pub over the years, but no one had ever seen anything like this. The level of violence was truly shocking. Some of them got up and left, but two brave souls approached McBride with the intention of halting the carnage. For a second he stopped and looked up at them with such venom that they immediately backed away and, leaving their drinks unfinished, they too left the pub.

The young woman serving had called her boss from the other bar. He immediately sent her to wait in the flat above and phoned for help. Ten minutes later two police officers arrived, followed by an ambulance from Lewisham hospital a few minutes later. McBride was standing at the bar nonchalantly sipping his beer by then. Sunshine was unconscious at his feet, his face a bloody mess. The crew of the ambulance could see he was badly injured but not critical. They loaded him on to a stretcher and took him off to hospital.

The police, meanwhile, arrested McBride, read him his rights, handcuffed him and took him outside. He was compliant and polite throughout. A police van arrived and he was taken away. The arresting officers went back into the pub and questioned the few customers who hadn't already left. They were not over surprised to find that nobody had seen or heard a thing. The landlord said he had been in the other bar and when he heard the commotion, had called the police but hadn't seen how it started. He didn't once mention the barmaid.

Pamment and Fenton followed the path for a few minutes. and then turned off and went deeper into the forest. Using powerful torches, they found what they were looking for, a small gap in the trees and a deep hole that had been prepared earlier. To begin with they had had to drag Kim, so Pamment had punched her and after that she was more compliant. It had stopped her whinging as well.

Pamment shone a light down into the hole, so she could see what was going to happen. Kim looked down into it and realised what they intended to do. Horror and fear invaded her body and mind, her eyes rolled up and she fell to the ground unconscious. The two men picked up the shovels that had been left for them and filled in the hole. They then covered the place with foliage and removed all signs of their presence. With nothing else to do they sat on a nearby log and waited. After ten minutes or so, Kim began to come to. She staggered to her feet, looked where the hole had been and felt totally confused. Then she saw Pamment and Fenton.

"Welcome back Kim," said Fenton, "I have a message from the boss. He wants you to know that despite the loathing he feels for you, you are still his wife and the mother of his children, so he is going to spare you this time. There's a bag for you over there. In it are some clothes, a train ticket to Liverpool and details of your new identity, Rachel Riches. There's also, a passport and driving licence in your new name and finally five thousand pounds in cash to get you started."

"I don't understand, what was the hole in the ground for?" asked Kim.

"Simple, if the boss ever sees or hears from you again, or you try to contact your children, he wants you to know that you will be in the hole next time, alive, when we bury you. Do you understand?" Kim nodded. "Good, we are going now. You are going to wait thirty minutes and then walk back to where we were parked, a car will come to take you to the station."

He handed her a torch, but as they began to walk away, Fenton turned.

"I think you are a very lucky woman Kim; I've never known Mr McBride act like this before. He's not exactly known for his forgiving nature. Don't blow it, and for fuck's sake don't drink the money away too quickly."

As they walked back, Pamment asked, "Why is the boss getting himself arrested, if she's not dead, I don't understand why he needs an alibi."

"God, you're thick sometimes," said Fenton, "He wants everyone to think she's dead, he's just making sure he doesn't get implicated. You can try someone for murder even if you haven't got a body you know."

When they got back in the car, they couldn't believe how hot it was.

"Bloody hell Barry, it's like a sauna in here, turn the heating off."

"Did you kill her, Kim? Did you?" asked Barry.

They could tell he was really emotional and they both wondered if he'd had some sort of relationship with her. They both decided not, he wouldn't have dared, surely.

Pamment answered with a smirk, "Won't be seeing her again."

Barry drove back to London, weeping silently.

Sunshine was in hospital for six days. He was concussed and had a broken nose, two broken ribs, a cracked cheek bone and was very badly bruised; his groin was painful for weeks. In all his years of boxing he had never been hit so hard nor sustained such serious injuries.

The police interviewed him but he said he had never met his attacker before; he thought the man must have been a racist who didn't like black people in his pub. He made it clear he would not press charges or give a statement. In the end the police told him to get lost. They contacted McBride, who had been given bail, and told him that they would not be charging him. The case was closed.

When Sunshine left hospital, he was surprised to find a taxi waiting for him. The driver took him home, and as he was about to get out, he handed him an envelope.

"The bloke who hired me told me to give you this package and he paid for the journey, so you don't owe me anything. Do you want me to help you in, you look a bit wobbly."

"No, you arright," said Sunshine.

"All right then, I'll leave you to it." He drove off.

Sunshine slowly and painfully climbed the stairs to his flat. He opened the package and inside was a note that said, 'You did well, you've earned a bonus. Now burn this note.' Also in the package was another five hundred pounds in tens. He burnt the paper and envelope and sat on his bed thinking about what had happened to him. He was grateful for the extra five hundred but surely the injuries he'd sustained and the pain he was in was worth more than a thousand pounds. He came to a decision; he was going to make sure he got at least another grand.

First though, he had to find out who the psycho was that had roughed him up and who the hell had employed him to do it. He took some pills the hospital had given him for the pain and managed to crawl into bed, even though every part of his body felt as if it had gone through a mangle. Despite his discomfort, he slept right through the night free from the depression and the bad thoughts that usually plagued him.

Harry had fallen asleep on the settee. Daniel often joked that he liked to have a short nap between his longer naps. Harry was a large, six year old Irish Setter, good natured, handsome and with a great temperament. However, when Daniel sneaked up on him and started brushing his fur and cutting out knots from under his armpits using scissors, Harry showed his displeasure by growling menacingly. Daniel took no notice; he knew the dog would never bite him, or anyone else for that matter. It greatly annoyed him that the vets at his practice were scared of him because of the growling and would never examine him without muzzling him first. Much to Harry's relief the phone rang and as Daniel went to answer it, the dog quickly sneaked out of the room and made his escape into the kitchen.

"Hello, oh hello Jake. How are you son? Great to hear from you ..... Yes, I know, I know, you're right I could ring you sometimes, not always leave it to you, you're right, but I'm a pensioner with no spare money for long distance phone calls, whereas you are a highly paid, skilled worker ...... Alright, so you're an arsonist, sorry I mean a fireman. Anyway, you know, I'm really busy ...... Retired! How dare you? I'm a full time, well known and successful author now, well will be, anytime soon. You know, three Completed books ...... Yes I know none of them have been published.

Anyway, I've sent the latest one to thirty agents. Surely one of them will take pity ..... Have I talked to who? ..... Tess? Your sister! You have a sister? Oh, of course, I remember. Small, pigtails, wears nappies ..... Jake, calm down, I talked to Tess on Tuesday and Jason yesterday and I was going to ring you tomorrow. I'll probably win the dad of the year award. The truth is you always get in first before I get the chance to ring you ..... No, nothing special, all quiet and dull here ..... Oh yes, Harry's fine. He's curled up next to me as we speak with his head resting on my lap and looking lovingly and respectfully up at me." Daniel glanced over to the far side of the room where Harry, thinking it was safe to return, had slunk back in and was fast asleep on one of the other chairs, as far away from Daniel and the scissors as possible ...... "OK, talk soon, love you, keep safe."

When Cora arrived at the address she had been given in Edgerton Road, Blackheath, she was pleased to see that the police were already there. She was getting really fed up with the verbal insults and abuse that she regularly received. Two months ago, she had been punched to the ground and kicked; it had shattered her confidence. She parked her car, got out, and shook hands with the officers.

"Hi, I'm Cora O'Brian, lead social worker in the children's unit."

"Nice to meet you Cora, I'm WPC Jean Virgin and my partner PC Peter Tagg. Nice house, in fact I reckon any one of them along here would cost a fortune."

"I think you're right. I don't think I'll be looking to buy one any time soon." said Cora, "So what's the problem here?"

"We've had a report of a child being abused. It was phoned in to the Lewisham nick anonymously," explained Tagg. "Our sergeant rang your lot and then sent us straight over as we were in the area. The caller said that the boy had been beaten and locked in a downstairs storage cupboard. He may have already been there some time. We've tried knocking but there doesn't seem to be anyone in."

"Of course, it could be a hoax," said Virgin, "we've had quite a few of them recently."

"Well, hoax or not, we need to get in and check, we can't risk waiting, I've got a small battering ram in the car, I'll get it," said Tagg.

The door was made of sturdy stuff and try as they might the battering ram was not big enough or strong enough to break it open. In the end they broke a window at the back of the house and Virgin climbed in and opened the door.

Once inside they walked up the hallway and soon came across a cupboard under the stairs. It had a bolt keeping it closed. Virgin opened the door and shone her torch inside. She saw a small boy cowering in a corner with his hands covering his face. He was shivering and was obviously cold and very frightened.

"Come on love, don't be scared, we're here to help you. Let's get you out of there." said Cora in a kind voice.

She very gently pulled him out, stood him up and took his hands in hers. It was the first time they had seen his face.

"Jesus Christ," said Tagg, "someone's given him a right going over."

Virgin glared at him.

Cora knelt down in front of him. "My names Cora sweetheart, what's your name? How old are you?"

The boy said nothing but started to cry. Cora hugged him and could smell urine on him. His shirt and trousers were filthy and he looked far too thin to be healthy. Tagg gave him a bottle of water. He grabbed it and gulped it down as fast as he could.

"Easy son, you'll choke doing that," he said, "just sip it, take your time."

They heard a noise behind them and turning round they saw a young girl standing watching them. She was very thin and looked around eight or nine years old. She had a pretty face, blond but rather dirty hair and was wearing black jeans and a blue T-shirt that could have done with a wash.

"Hello lovely, what's your name?" asked Cora.

"Zeta," She said, "he's my brother."

"How old are you both Zeta?"

"He's six and I'm nine."

"And what's your brother's name, Zeta."

"Eddie."

"Do you know what happened to him Zeta? Who locked him in the cupboard?" asked Virgin.

She shook her head and looked away. She went over to her brother and took his hand.

"Zeta, are you two alone or is there someone else in the house?" asked Tagg. She shook her head. "All right, look, you two take them back to the station. I'll have a quick look round the house and then follow you in the panda. I expect there'll be a bit of paperwork and then you can take them somewhere safe."

Chapter 3 Jackie

Daniel Pitt was surprised when he received a phone call from an old friend he had not heard from for a few months, Jackie Wentworth. She wanted them to meet up. She was a police officer and had recently been promoted to Inspector. He was sure she must be an amazing and well respected officer. A woman reaching that level of command was still quite rare all around the country and she was one of only a few who had made it to detective inspector level in the Somerset and Avon force.

Daniel had got to know Jackie through teaching both her children maths. She was a police constable at the time, based in Taunton but living in Cheddar in a house she had inherited from her aunt. She'd gone as a parent helper on a six day school trip that Daniel had run to La Clusaz in the Alps. She was in her late twenties at the time and he'd discovered she had a great sense of humour. Daniel had liked her from the minute they'd met. Being a police officer, she had a slightly cynical view of the world and those in it. This suited Daniel's sense of humour perfectly.

She had been really good with the pupils in France. They all seemed to like her and, wherever she went, she always seemed to have an entourage of children following her. Even more useful was that she spoke fluent French and German.

On a day trip to Annecy, many of the pupils had gone swimming in the lake and were playing around in the water, jumping off a large wooden cross that was about fifty metres from the shore. Daniel was worried as the lifeguard did not seem to be particularly vigilant, indeed he seemed to spend most of the time observing the many topless women lying sunbathing on the shore. Mind you, so were some of the boys from his party. Despite their young age, some of them seemed to have their tongues hanging out. Still, they had probably, literally, never seen anything quite like it before.

He was about to call the pupils back to the shore when Jackie, who had obviously come to the same conclusion concerning the children's safety, quickly changed into her swimsuit. Without being asked, she swam out to the cross and took control, ensured that everyone was safe. She invented and joined in the games and the pupils loved it. She even included French children and those on holiday from other countries. It was a really happy scene. That was the sort of person she was.

They met at Daniel's local; The Shipham Inn in the village of that name. It lay on top of an escarpment nestled on the edge of the Mendip Hills in Somerset. Daniel went to the bar to buy a half pint of bitter for each of them and Jackie walked over to some comfy seats positioned around a roaring fire. She was about to sit down when Daniel called her away and they settled down in a quiet corner on the far side of the pub.

"So, you don't want me to be warm and comfy then," said Jackie, a little cross.

At that moment the door opened and four old timers walked in. They were dressed in old muddy boots, frayed trousers held up with string and coats that looked as if they had seen better days. They all wore caps or woolly hats. They made their way straight to the fireside seats and settled down. The landlord had their pints of raw local cider ready and took them over.

"So, why should four local yokels have precedence over a very important and well respected police officer. I've a good mind to arrest them for being scruffy without a license."

"Well, if there was a very important and well respected police officer around, perhaps things might be different. The fact is they have been sitting in those seats every evening for the last thirty years, and before that, their dads sat in the same place. And I'll tell you something else, if you did arrest and interview them, you wouldn't understand a word they said; they speak old Mendip, it's a different language."

"OK, I'll let them off this time. So, how's retirement, I've got to say you look good on it."

"I feel very good, and how about you, Detective Inspector Jackie Wentworth? Look I'm sorry I didn't call to congratulate you. You know how it is."

"Don't worry, I have caller ID, I wouldn't have answered anyway. You know I was thinking the other day, how you and I became pals. I think we really got to know each other on that school trip to France."

"That's right." Daniel thought for a few seconds. "You were a great person to have along, always full of good ideas. The best one was how to deal with mealtimes, especially dinner in the evenings".

"Oh God, yes," said Jackie, "The children had the most appalling manners I had ever seen. And the noise they made was unbearable, it was like they were having a competition, who could shout the loudest, I was really shocked. They lounged on the table, ate with their fingers; they were disgusting, it was like being at the chimpanzee's dinner party."

Daniel laughed, "I think you're being a bit unfair on chimpanzees. Anyway, on the third evening you'd had enough. You stood up and smashed your truncheon down on the table. You never did tell me why you had that with you."

"Never go anywhere without it. Anyway, I told them that in order to improve their French, during dinner times they could only speak to each other, en langue française and anyone who broke the rule would lose half what was left of their pocket money."

"Brilliant, simply brilliant. Dinner times were totally silent for the remainder of the trip, not a peep."

They both sat in silence for a minute or two lost in their own memories.

"What was your most embarrassing moment as a teacher?" asked Jackie.

"That's easy, we were taking one hundred third year pupils on a trip to London for five days. At the pre-trip meeting with parents, one of them asked if we had a plan in case we were caught somewhere in the city where an suspected act of terrorism was taking place.

I said, 'Absolutely, without any panicking we would walk briskly, but calmly, away from the incident until we found a safe place to be or a police officer who could advise us. Oh, then we'd probably go back and fetch the pupils.' I remember pausing so that everybody could laugh at my clever and witty sense of humour, but there was nothing, not even a titter, just silence as a hundred and fifty people, all stared at me, wondered if I was fit to be put in charge of a group of children and whether they should risk allowing their precious offspring to go. The only person in the hall who wasn't staring at me was the head, he had his face in his hands. My sense of humour regularly gets me into hot water. What about you?"

Jackie was chuckling. "Brilliant, love it, just the sort of daft thing you would say. Mine was probably when I was with my partner patrolling in Bridgwater, it was about ten at night. As we passed an alley way I saw a bloke with his back to us doing something to a woman. I got out the car but when I got near it was obvious there was no problem, they were more than likely just canoodling. So, I shouted that they should find a hotel or go home and not have sex in public; I didn't say it in a serious way. Anyway, he pushed her further into the alley and came out looking very red faced and aggressive. That's when I recognised him, it was only the chief superintendent in charge of CID for Avon and Somerset. He was old school, believed women should be in the kitchen, certainly not in a police uniform. Anyway, he told me his wife had something in her eye and he was trying to get it out.

"I got a right bollocking, he accused me of being unprofessional and harassing innocent people, rudeness to members of the public and plenty more. He said I would be hearing more about this in the coming days."

"And did he follow it up?"

"He couldn't really," she smiled, "you see, whoever it was in that alleyway, it wasn't his wife, I had met her before."

They sat quietly for a few seconds. Daniel was looking at her but she wouldn't look up from her drink and meet his eye.

"I have this slight tingly feeling that this invitation to have a drink was not just a catchup. Am I right Detective Inspector Wentworth. Come on, spit it out."

"I am truly in awe of your ability to smell a rat. You should be a police officer." She smiled and then looked serious. "Look, truth is, I need a favour, quite a big favour actually, as it happens."

"Oh God strike me down. Go on."

"I need someone to look after two children, just for a short while."

Daniel looked at her as if she was stir crazy and laughed. "Are you kidding, you know I don't do children."

"How can you say that you have three of your own and you were a great teacher, everybody said so. A legend. Look this is going to sound melodramatic but the truth is these kids are in a spot of bother. I just need them out of the way for a few days."

"I was never a great teacher; but what I was, was really good at making other people think that I was a great teacher. Anyway, I hate kids and the answer is a definitive and categorical no."

"Look, their father is a really violent man. I just need you to have them for a week or so, to get them out of the way while we sort out the legalities," said Jackie.

"Ha! I notice a few days has just become a week or so. Why can't they go into a foster home; you must have emergency places for kids like that."

"No, we can't do that. OK, I'm going to tell you the whole story. Let me get you another drink."

"Thanks, I'll have a treble strychnine with a dash of Valium."

Jackie went to the bar with their glasses and asked for two more halves of bitter. She brought them back to the table and moved her chair so she was sitting next to Daniel. She spoke quietly.

"The children are nine and six. Their father's name is Justin McBride. He trades in violence which he sells to anyone who can afford it. He works for some of the most vicious gangs in London. I have a friend who works undercover for the Met. He reckons McBride is the nastiest piece of work he's ever come across; he just loves seeing people suffer. The problem is, it's not only criminal gangs he's worked for in the past. My friend believes he gets protection from high ranking officers in the Met and other forces. I'm not saying they use his services, but somehow he's able to put pressure on them. Anyway, there was a serious incident and social services removed the children, who were alone in their house, and took them into care. Then through various links, which I don't really want to go into, the problem became mine. The worry is, if they go to a listed safe house, he will use his contacts to get information and get to them. So, I have been asked to find somewhere safe for them that only I will know about."

"But surely there's a paper trail. If he's got the sort of connections that you're talking about, then he's bound to find out where they've gone."

"No," said Jackie, "there is no paper trail. Only one person in the met knows I am involved, and no one apart from me will know where I am going to put them."

"This sounds really dodgy to me, is it even legal?"

"Well, that's the problem, I don't really know, I'm not even sure that the way they were removed was OK, but believe me, it had to be done."

"I'm sure I'm going to regret asking this," said Daniel, "why were they removed?"

"Their names are Zeta, she's nine years old and Eddie, who's six. Last Thursday, it seems that Eddie did something wrong, we don't know what, it really doesn't matter. Anyway, his dad threw him into a small cupboard with no light and left him for five hours, five hours! Can you believe that? When the boy was released, he asked for some water. His dad beat the shit out of him and threw him back in the cupboard. Altogether, he was in there for eight hours without food or water. Someone rang the police; we don't know who. A social worker and two police officers broke into the house, removed the children and took them to the local nick, Lewisham. Look, this is a photo of Eddie when they found him."

Daniel looked at the photograph. He grimaced and couldn't believe what he was seeing.

"Bloody hell, that's awful, surely you can throw his dad in jail for that."

"According to McBride, he wasn't even near the place, and plenty of witnesses will back him up. There was a babysitter who should have been there. Eddie was playing in the garden. Apparently, a crazy thug who was passing beat him up. He was so upset he hid in a cupboard and accidently locked himself in. And guess what, there's a girl who swears she was supposed to be babysitting. She says she fell ill and went home."

"Surely the boy told you what really happened."

"Daniel, he's six years old. The truth is, Eddie wants his dad to love him, but he's also terrified of him. Every time he told us what happened, the story changed and he never once mentioned his dad doing anything wrong. Zeta refuses to talk about it. We think she's telling Eddie do the same. We strongly suspect that Zeta has been sexually abused by him in the past, she kind of indicated that, but then clammed up and wouldn't say anything more. The truth is, a court would never accept Eddie's story, It's too confusing."

"What a mess, Is there a mum?"

"Their mum's name was Kim. She wasn't much to write home about, but that was probably not her fault, she was controlled and abused by McBride as much as the kids were. Apparently, she had contacted an aunt in Stoke and asked to stay with her for a short while with the two children. The theory is that McBride somehow found out and killed her, or more likely had her killed by one of his lackies. The trouble is we never found the body. We did an exhaustive search and turned up nothing, everybody involved with his gang had a watertight alibi, and McBride was in a police cell for beating someone up in a pub. I don't think you can get a better alibi than that. I mean it's possible she's still alive somewhere but personally, I'm ninety nine percent sure she's dead. Look, I'm sorry, I'm not meaning to frighten you."

"Well, you're doing a bloody good job. Did McBride say anything at all."

"Oh yes," said Jackie, "he said he had suspected she was seeing another man and thinks they ran off together. As if she would dare!"

She took a sip of her drink and was quiet for a few seconds.

"Daniel, I need to tell you, there is one other thing you should know. My friend in the Met says there is a rumour going round that McBride has put the word out that he's gonna hurt anyone involved in keeping his kids away from him."

"Hurt? Hurt how?" asked Daniel.

"Well, to be honest, more sort of kill, actually."

"Right, so let me sum up. I, who as everyone knows, have a pathological hatred for children, apart from my own, and even them I can only tolerate in very short bursts, get to have two of them, in my house, interrupting my peace and serenity. And what is my reward for this act of kindness and good will, torture for the main course and then death for dessert. You should take up a career in public relations."

Daniel looked at the photograph. “I must be crazy,” he said putting his head in his hands.

Chapter 4 The Arrival

Two days later, Jackie was parked in the main car park at Membury Services on the M4. It was around ten o'clock at night and fully dark. She was anxiously watching the entrance to the car park. Finally, she saw the Ford Escort Hatchback arrive. It had been borrowed from the police pound and fitted with false plates. After what felt to her like a long wait, the car pulled up beside her and a man jumped out, he opened the backdoor and two children got out and immediately climbed into Jackie's borrowed car.

Without speaking to them she pulled away heading west. As she passed the service's petrol station, a police Vauxhall Omega, with two officers on board, pulled out behind and followed her. As Jackie left the service station to join the slip road taking her onto the motorway, the officers behind her switched on their blue flashing light and pulled across the road, blocking access to the M4. One of the policemen got out and explained to motorists behind that there had been an incident on the motorway but it would only be a short wait.

After ten minutes they moved out of the way and allowed the traffic through. Jackie, meanwhile, had sped west down the motorway for about three miles until she saw a Citroen BX Estate parked in the safety lane. She pulled in behind it and bundled the children into the back seat of the Citroen. Without acknowledging the driver, she returned to her car. The Austin pulled away but Jackie remained where she was for a further fifteen minutes and then headed back to Somerset.

Daniel could make out the shapes of the two children huddled together on the back seat.

"Hi kids," he said in his child friendliest voice, "I'm Daniel, I want you to try and relax and get some sleep if you can. The journey will be about two hours. In the pouch in front of you is some water, a few bags of crisps and a couple of chocolate bars just in case you're hungry or thirsty. I'll put on some great music for you to enjoy."

He pushed a cassette into the machine and fell under the spell of his favourite artist, Al Stewart, singing Bedsitter Images. Nobody evoked life in London as a young man in the seventies like Stewart.

He didn't rush and kept a little under the speed limit. The children in the back remained silent for the whole journey. Daniel could sense their tension; they had no idea where they were going or what was going to happen to them.

It was a clear night and the moon was full, and at one point, Danniel told them to look out of their left side window.

"You can just make out a range of hills in the distance, that's the Mendip Hills. My house is on the edge of those."

Twenty five minutes later they arrived at Daniel's cosy three bedroom cottage in Shipham. The village was split into two parts and Daniel lived in Upper Shipham. He ushered the children in and took them through to the living room and sat them down on the settee. He lit the gas fire to warm the room and then went through to the kitchen leaving the door open.

"OK, this is your home for a short while." he called out. "There's a very nice garden out back, you'll see it tomorrow. There are sheep and lambs in the field behind and sometimes horses. I thought you might like to try horse riding while you're here, there are lots of stables around. I know this is really difficult for you, but all I can say is you're safe here. You're in the village of Shipham and only nice things happen here, never any nasty things. We are only three miles from a place called Cheddar. You might have heard of it; it has a famous gorge." He waited to see if anyone would answer but they were silent. "Amazingly it's called Cheddar Gorge. It has caves as well, they're quite famous. Anyway, a hundred years ago the good fairy of Shipham beat the bad fairy of Cheddar at a game of tiddlywinks and made a spell that nothing bad could ever happen in our village. Put your hands up all those who believe me."

Eddie was sitting as close to Zeta as he could. He started to put his hand up but Zeta stopped him. Daniel put his head round the door and sighed loudly and made a funny face when he saw that no one had their hand in the air. Eddie giggled, but Zeta nudged him to stop.

"Come and sit at the table in the kitchen. There's some homemade tomato soup, lovely fresh white bread and delicious butter, and It's very important for you to know that everything you are about to eat was grown by me, here in my garden."

"You grew the butter?" asked Eddie, with a great deal of astonishment.

"Of course, my butter tree is one of the finest in Somerset."

The children nibbled at their food but did not eat a great deal. It did not surprise Daniel as they had scoffed all the chocolate and crisps within a few minutes of getting in the car. It was the first time Daniel had had the opportunity to look at them close up. Zeta was a very pretty girl. She was tall and slim with long blond hair hanging freely round her shoulders. Her face, whilst being pleasing to look at, had a feral look about it, as if nothing and no-one could be trusted; she looked as if she could only survive on her own wits, everyone else was shut out. Eddie was thin, much too thin. He had a mop of brown hair, inexpertly cut with a pudding bowl fringe at the front. He had a sweet face but also fear and sadness in his eyes. He needed to be loved and did not understand the world he lived in. It seemed to Daniel that Eddie was desperate to find someone he could trust, whereas Zeta knew she never would. Looking at them made Daniel feel sad but also determined to give the children some fun while they were with him, make them both realise that not everyone and everything was bad.

"I had to think of made up names for you to have while you're here. I hope you don't mind. I chose Ben and Lucy Hempleman. So, you must get used to calling each other those."

Zeta frowned, "I don't like the name Lucy."

"I know, I'm really sorry but I couldn't ask you, I had to decide on the names before I met you. I've told my neighbours you're my niece's children from Swindon. She had to go away for a while."

"But that's a lie, my mummy told me not to lie," said Eddie.

"Your mummy was quite right Eddie, but the exception is if you do it to keep nice children safe, OK? The thing is it's really important that no one at all knows who you really are. Anyway, you've got to forget your old names, You're now Ben and Lucy.

"Are you going to eat anymore? No. OK, come on, I'll show you to your bedroom, I didn't think you'd mind sharing."

"My mummy's dead," said Ben, who was trying to hold back tears.

"Yes, I know, I'm really sorry Ben." Daniel squeezed his shoulder.

They went upstairs with Ben staying as close to Lucy as he could.

Daniel had spent the last two days making the spare bedroom as child friendly as possible. He'd done a really good job; each wall had been painted a different bright colour and he'd bought pyjamas, a continental quilt and pillow slips for the double bed with pictures of animals all over. He had also scoured the local charity shops for books and games. In the corner was a large box and in it were lots of toys, mainly cuddly animals.

"The bathroom's there, there's everything you need; you know, toothbrushes, towels, flannels and all that kind of stuff. Lucy, will you give Ben a hand please? I'll wait in my bedroom, over there. Call me when you're in bed and I'll come and say goodnight."

Daniel sat on his bed and carried on talking while they were getting ready.

"Those toys in the box belonged to my three kids, hopefully you'll meet them sometime, they smell a bit, but they're OK. The toys, not the kids. Although, now I come to think about it, the kids are quite smelly as well. The toys were in a box in the garage, it took me ages to find them. We used to tell stories using them. They're too old for that now, all in their twenties and thirties.

"You'll like Shipham. That's the village we're in. It's got a butchers and general store, a school, a church, a pub, a post office, a square, and a football pitch. Oh, and a pond. Everyone's very friendly. There are lots of woods and fields nearby."

"We're ready," called out Lucy, "Ben wants the light left on, he's scared of the dark."

Daniel walked in and saw both children on their backs with the quilt pulled right up to their chins.

"Of course, I'll leave the door open and the landing light on. By the way, I don't know if you're into reading, but if you look over there at the bookcase, I've been buying books from charity shops and stuff that I thought you might like. The bottom shelf is for Ben and the second one up belongs to you Lucy. Anyway, I'll see you in the morning, goodnight."

He looked across Lucy to where Ben was lying, he could see he was distraught and obviously something was really worrying him.

"What's up Ben?" he said, trying to be gentle and soothing.

Ben burst into uncontrollable sobs.

"Lucy, do you know why he's crying."

"He's scared." said Lucy.

"Please stay with us." Ben managed to say through the tears.

Daniel thought for a moment.

"OK, Lucy, swap places with Ben. I am going to get a chair and sleep right here in the doorway, Is that OK, Ben?" He nodded. "Lucy, I won't come further into the room, I promise. Now, go to sleep, it's after midnight and we have to be up early as my very important lodger will be arriving first thing, and he will be very anxious to meet you both."

Ben, who was already feeling safer, said, "What's a lodger?"

"Someone who stays in your house," replied Daniel.

"Who is it?" asked Lucy, looking a little concerned.

"Aha, you'll have to wait and see, but I promise you'll like him. See you in the morning."

A few hours later, Daniel woke up with a start, he felt very stiff from sleeping in the chair; it was incredibly uncomfortable. Something had woken him but it took him a few seconds to work out what it was. He looked over and could see Lucy was sitting up, and Ben was lying on his front, whimpering into his pillow.

"What's wrong Ben, what is it? Ben, tell me what's wrong. Lucy, do you know?"

"He's wet the bed; he's frightened you're going to be mad; shout at him and beat him up."

Daniel sat on the bed and took hold of Ben's hand.

"Now, you listen to me young man," he said in a soft and what he hoped was a reassuring voice, "in this house, beating people up is not allowed, nor has it ever been. And I will also tell you that no one will hurt you or shout at you, ever, for whatever reason. I promise, scout's honour. The thing is, lots of people wet the bed, I did when I was your age, it wasn't my fault and it isn't your fault, it just happens. Now, I have a ten point plan for dealing with wet beds. I call it, 'the ten point plan for dealing with wet beds!' One, leap out of bed. Two, a quick change of jama bottoms. Three, a quick change of jama tops, if necessary. Four, we change the sheet. Five, first thing in the morning, you take the wet things down and chuck them in the washing machine. I'll show you where that is tomorrow. So, let's get going. Ben, change into those, and Lucy help me put the clean sheet on."

"I thought you said it was a ten point plan," said Lucy.

"I didn't say that did I Ben?"

"Yes, you did, you said ten."

"You traitor Ben, I've a good mind to nibble your kneecaps as a punishment. Anyway, ten was an estimate."

"You're stupid," said Lucy.

Daniel clutched his heart as if mortally wounded and then had to explain to Ben what an estimate meant. In the end he wished he'd kept his sense of humour to himself. However, his strategy was to try to get the two of them engaging with him and it was working to some extent. Eventually, Daniel and the children, who were both far more of a hindrance than a help, got Ben and the bed sorted. Ben was asleep almost as soon as his head hit the pillow. Daniel stroked his head.

"Night night, sweet dreams. Goodnight Lucy."

Lucy turned away from him, closed her eyes and didn't say anything. He was a man, and men could not be trusted, ever.

Chapter 5 Harry the Hunter

Lucy and Ben woke to the sound of the doorbell ringing. Lucy looked around. She knew Daniel had been in the room, the curtains had been drawn back and sunshine was streaming in. Also, the bedroom door had been closed. Both children listened carefully. They could hear voices and a sort of scuffling noise downstairs. Ben looked very anxious. After a minute or two, they could hear footsteps coming up the stairs and another sound. There was scratching on the outside of the door. Both children sat up and pulled the bed clothes around them, not knowing what to expect. Ben took Lucy's hand. The door opened. A handsome, hairy and very large Irish Setter leapt into the room, jumped on the bed, and made a huge fuss of both children, licking their faces and climbing all over them. His tail was wagging so hard the children had to use their arms to protect their faces. He had wonderful soft fur, the colour of autumn ferns, and he tore around like a mad thing, jumping on and off the bed. At one point, he jumped down to the floor and rushed round and round trying to catch his own tail. The children loved it and tried to hug and stroke him. Finally, after five or so minutes of absolute chaos, everything calmed down and the dog collapsed and lay down between the children, panting and exhausted and enjoyed multiple tickles to his ears and tummy.

"Ben and Lucy," said Daniel, proudly, "meet Harry, my lodger and best friend. Now, you two get dressed while

I get your breakfast. We will then take Harry onto the hills for his morning constitutional."

"His what?" asked Ben.

"He means walk." said Lucy.

"I do indeed, but always remember Ben, never use a short word if you can think of a longer and more complicated one, especially one that other people don't understand."

"You're bonkers," said Lucy.

After their breakfast of marmalade on toast and orange juice, Daniel bundled them all into his Citroen Estate; the children in the back and Harry in the boot and drove to a small nearby hamlet called Charterhouse, where he parked the car at the side of the road. Daniel led them through a stile and let Harry off the lead in a place called Ubley Warren. It was a huge area, quite flat in parts but with some steep hilly sections. It was perfect for dog walking; the whole area was enclosed with fencing and there was no possibility of a dog running off and getting lost. Not that that was a problem with Harry, he always made sure Daniel was in sight. Daniel explained that they were right on top of the Mendip Hills, Shipham was on the edge of them. He made them stand still and look at the magnificent view all round. Even Lucy was impressed.

There were lots of trees in the area and many had white blossom. There was purple gorse and many types of wildflowers. There were also many dips and mounds and Daniel explained that the local name for this sort of feature was gruffy ground, the remains of mining activity. It was an

AONB, an area of outstanding natural beauty, which meant nobody could come along and build on it.

"It's a really beautiful place," said Lucy.

Daniel agreed, "yes, it is."

The children chased after Harry and threw sticks for him. He always ran after them but then lost interest and went for a sniff. Ben ran back to Daniel and took his hand.

"He has a job you know, Harry. He's known as Harry the hunter," said Daniel.

"What does he hunt?" asked Ben.

"Elephants."

Ben looked very surprised.

"How does he hunt elephants?"

"Well, he jumps on their backs and licks their ears. Now elephants are very ticklish, especially around the ears. So, they laugh so much that they start to shake and wobble and finally they fall over."

"Then what happens?"

"We cook the elephant and eat it."

Ben looked shocked.

"You can't eat an elephant."

"Of course you can."

"How?" asked Ben

"Well, you pop down to the co-op and buy some bread and butter, butter two slices of the bread and put the elephant between them, and then, Bob's your uncle, you have an elephant sandwich."

Lucy had run up and was listening carefully to the conversation.

"I thought you said you grew the butter in your garden."

"Ah, that's true, I do, but elephants are allergic to garden grown butter, they come out in a rash, so, I have to buy it,"

"He's lying Ben."

Daniel clutched his chest and fell to the floor lying on his back. He opened his eyes and winked at Ben. Ben burst out laughing and then ran off to chase after Harry. He tried unsuccessfully to interest him in chasing another stick.

"How are you doing, Lucy?" Daniel asked.

"I don't like the name Lucy." Said Lucy petulantly.

"I'm sorry, but how are you doing anyway?"

"OK."

Daniel had the impression she was far from OK, but she didn't say any more. Instead, she ran after Ben and Harry. Ben was fighting a losing battle trying to catch Harry and finally gave up and skidded up to Daniel.

"I like Harry, he's handsome."

"That's why he's called Handsome Harry," said Daniel.

"I thought he was called Harry the Hunter," said Ben, looking confused.

"That's right, Handsome Harry the Hunter."

Lucy ran up looking worried.

"There's another dog over there, Harry's gone to see it."

"That's OK," said Daniel, "that's Micky, known as Tricky Micky."

"Why is he called Tricky Micky?" asked Lucy.

"Well, his name is Micky and he's tricky."

"You're stupid," snarled Lucy.

They walked on. Ben took Daniel's hand, Lucy walked the other side of him, keeping her distance.

"Have you ever had pets?"

"Mummy bought me a hamster once."

Daniel could see tears welling up in his eyes, he feared the worst and wished he hadn't asked.

"When dad came home, he flushed it down the toilet." said Lucy in a quiet voice.

Daniel squeezed Ben's hand in what he hoped was a supportive way.

They came across a hillock, and Daniel told them about a game he used to play with his own children on this very spot. It was called 'king of the hill'. Actually, it wasn't quite true, the game had always taken place on a different hill, some way away, but he thought the story might stop Ben dwelling on his hamster.

"I used to lie on the hill, pretending to be asleep. They had to get me off and take over the hill."

"Did they win?" asked Ben.

"Never, I used to fling them in every direction. To be honest, it was quite a dangerous game.

"Do you still play?"

"Heavens, no. As soon as they got big enough to have a chance of winning, I stopped playing. They would have been a lot less gentle with me than I was with them. And I wasn't that gentle."

"Can we play now?" asked Ben.

"No, not now. Perhaps another time."

"Why not?"

"Well, just at the moment, I'm recovering from two broken legs, a broken arm and a fingernail that needs cutting."

Lucy raised her eyebrows and told him again that he was stupid. She ran off to play with Harry but Ben was in two minds as to what to do. He decided he would stay with Daniel for a while.

Leaving Charterhouse, Daniel took a different route home. He took them to the top of Cheddar Gorge and drove slowly down. He stopped at one point and let them out of the car to see the famous Lion Rock, and the huge cliffs towering either side of the gorge.

"So, the whole gorge is made up of one type of rock called limestone. Now, Cheddar Gorge was once a cave, and over millions of years the river that flowed through here ate away at the rock and formed this shape. Then at some point in the past the roof collapsed and left this. When that happens the thing that is left is called a gorge.

Ben, who hadn't really understood much of what Daniel had said, asked, "where is the river now?"

"Under you. It still flows down the gorge but underground. This area has lots of caves, called potholes. People go into them to explore. It's a popular pastime in this area. I used to do it myself."

They drove to the bottom of the gorge and stopped in front of some shops. Daniel pointed out a fast river flowing past.

"That's the river from under the gorge. It's called the River Yeo. Strange really because yeo is local language for river, so it's actually called River River."

That evening, the children were sitting at the table waiting for their tea. Daniel had cooked the sort of thing he thought kids would probably like, a burger, chips and peas. He put their dinner in front of each of them and noted neither of them thanked him. He returned to the kitchen to fetch his, and when he re-entered, he nearly dropped his plate. He was absolutely horrified at what he was seeing. Both children had covered their food with tomato ketchup and were lounging with their elbows on the table and eating with their fingers. Not only that but they were chewing with their mouths wide open and making the most disgusting noise. Even Harry looked shocked.

"**STOP**!" He said.

Both children froze and looked at him with a look of alarm.

"I honestly thought I was at the zoo when I walked in." He forced himself to calm down and lower his tone. "You two make Harry's eating habits look sophisticated."

They all looked over at Harry, who fortunately, didn't appear to have taken offence.

"Now on Saturday," continued Daniel, "I am taking you to a Chinese restaurant for the best sweet and sour pork in the world, no, in the universe, but you cannot eat the way you are now, goodness no. You would cause a riot and I would be banned from ever going there again.

"Now look, Saturday is four days away, so I will teach you one table manner every day until then. If you do it properly each of you will get twenty pence every day and if you manage in the restaurant you will get a bonus of fifty pence. Is that a deal?

"Yes." shouted Ben enthusiastically.

Daniel and Ben both looked at Lucy who was sullenly forking her tomato ketchup.

"Lucy?" said Daniel.

"Suppose so." she replied with a defiant tone.

"Did no-one ever teach you eating manners?"

"I don't remember. I think we usually ate on our own," said Ben.

"OK, we start with using the knife and fork. Are you both right handed. OK, good, hold your knife in the right hand and fork in the left, hold them like this. Fantastic. Stick your fork in the burger to hold it steady, now cut with the knife. Pick the piece up with the fork and pop it into your mouth. Now spear one chip, one chip lucy, not twenty one, and into your mouth. Finally, you use your knife to push a few peas onto your fork and take the fork to your mouth. OK, now do it yourself, burger first, then a chip, then some peas."

They both managed to do it, rather awkwardly but correctly.

"Excellent, well done, once more."

They repeated the exercise several times.

"Good, here's your twenty pence. I'll take you to the sweet shop in the morning so that you can spend it. We will do another table manner tomorrow but you must keep using what you learned today. Was that OK, Ben?"

"I'm going to buy an ice cream, thanks Daniel."

Daniel looked at Lucy. "Lucy?"

"It was bollocks." Lucy got up, pushed her plate onto the floor, knocked her chair over and walked out. Daniel didn't go after her, 'small steps' he thought.

Lucy expected Daniel to chase after her and tell her off for her behaviour, she really felt in the mood for an argument. But he didn't, he let her go. She didn't know what to make of it. Her past experiences of men had led her to assume all of them were hateful, but Daniel did seem to be different. That didn't mean she was going to trust him though. Despite her tantrum, he continued to speak to her in a kind way, he never shouted at her, got angry or tried to make her talk about things she didn't want to.

Later that evening, after they had played a few games of snap, Daniel asked them to go and get ready for bed. Even though her first instinct was to get stroppy and argue, she managed to control herself and do as Daniel said. Her father never asked, he told, and if you weren't quick to obey you were liable to get thumped in the head.

When they were ready, Daniel asked if they wanted a bedtime story. Ben, of course, was hugely enthusiastic but Lucy decided to say nothing, and ignore Daniel for the rest of the evening.

Daniel went to the toy box and took out a selection of furry animals to help him tell the story. As he had done with his own kids, he intended to make it up as he went along; the use of the animals and their different voices was integral.

He told the children how Eli the elephant and Humphrey the Hippo were enjoying a very tasty cream tea at Eli's cottage. Ben had immediately interrupted.

""What's a cream tea?"

"Ah, now a cream tea is when you have scones, they are a sort of sweet, delicious tasting bread and you eat them with clotted cream and jam." explained Daniel.

"That sounds fantastic, I've never had one of those. Can we have one Daniel?" said Ben.

"Tell you what, we will have a cream tea tomorrow," said Daniel.

Daniel continued the story and explained that Bobby the bear had knocked on Eli's door to tell him that Roger Rabbit had been kidnapped by the evil and cunning, Colin Crocodile and Dino Dinosaur. This worried Ben and he intervened once more.

"A dinosaur, that's very scary. Was it a terracotta rex?"

"Tyrannosaurus rex, you idiot!" said Lucy.

Daniel continued, explaining that Eli and Humphrey had set off to rescue Roger with the help of their friends Tommy the tiger and Tommy the lion.

Colin and Dino had Roger tied up in a sack but they told Eli and Humphrey that they were actually making turnip soup and that they hadn't seen Reggie all day. Unbeknown to them, Tommy and Tommy, replaced Roger with some very heavy stones. Daniel continued.

"When Eli and Humphrey had gone, Colin said, 'we fooled them, we are so very, very clever.' 'Clever, intelligent and sophisticated, that's us,' said Dino, doing a little jig.

"They picked up the sack and were both very surprised how heavy Reggie was. 'Reggie must eat an awful lot of ... whatever it is that rabbits eat' said Dino. After a great deal of effort, they managed to get the sack high enough to tip the contents into the pot. When the rocks hit the boiling water some of it splashed over them and they both screamed and made an awful fuss. 'Oooo, it hurts, it hurts,' yelled Dino. 'Mine hurts even more,' shouted Colin. They ran down to the river, arguing as to who was in the worst pain and jumped in. The water was very cold and murky. Eli, Humphrey, Tommy, Tommy and Reggie all stood on the bank and laughed and cheered. They could hear Colin moaning about being very wet, and Dino saying he was even wetter. 'Let's hope that will teach them a lesson.' said Eli, 'Now we'll go to my house and we'll all have a nice cup of tea and a slice of my extra special lemon drizzle cake.' The end."

"That was nice, I enjoyed that. Were they badly burnt, Colin and Dino?" asked Ben.

"No, they were fine, just a bit cold, wet and singed. I expect they had turnip soup for supper. Would you like to have one of the animals to take to bed with you, Ben?"

"Yes please. Could I have Tommy the tiger?"

"Sure. Would you like one Lucy?"

Lucy shook her head. "It doesn't make any sense!"

"What doesn't?" asked Daniel.

"Why would a crocodile be upset about jumping in a river and getting wet, they live in rivers and lakes?"

Daniel laughed. "Very well observed, but, I have to warn you, you'll be Lucy no-mates if you try to be too clever. Now sleep."

"There were no girls." said Lucy thoughtfully.

"What?"

"All the animals were boys, there were no girls."

This came as a bomb shell to Daniel.

"Good heavens, you're right. Do you know I never realised? There will be girls in the next story, I promise. I wonder if Eli could be a girl's name. He could become Elly."

Ben asked Daniel if he would stay and Daniel told him he would be up later.

"Can Harry stay?"

"No, he finds humans too dirty to sleep with. He did ask me to ask you both a favour though. He says, very unfairly in my opinion, that I sometimes forget to feed him after his walks, so he wants Ben to feed him in the morning and Lucy in the evening, what do you think about that?"

Both Lucy and Ben said they would, and Ben gave Daniel and Harry a hug. Lucy just hugged Harry.

That night, Ben wet the bed once again and Daniels ten point plan became a fifteen point plan. However, now Ben knew that he needn't worry about it and he would not get into trouble, going to bed became far less stressful. He wet the bed twice more in the next five nights, but after that, he hardly ever did it again.

By the end of the week, the children had done reasonably well with their lessons in table manners, but, as they entered the Riverside Chinese restaurant at the bottom of Cheddar Gorge, Daniel was still a worried man. They sat down and Daniel noticed there were chopsticks laid out on the table and no other cutlery. Daniel beckoned the waiter over.

"Kwok, could the children have knives and forks please?"

"Mr P, how long you been coming here. You should know, only chopsticks, no knives, no forks."

He started to giggle. Daniel didn't know what was going on, then he turned and looked over to Ben and Lucy. Both children were looking at him with a big smirk on their faces, with chopsticks hanging out of their noses. Daniel did his best to look cross and not to laugh.

After apologising to Kwok. Daniel decided to abandon the idea of Chinese and picked up fish and chips on the way home. He told them both they could eat it from the paper with their fingers and they both made sure they ate as badly as they possibly could. Daniel could see Lucy was enjoying the joke, and that, at least, was good to see.

Chapter 6 Sunshine

Sunshine Mawa had been born in a three bedroom tenement flat on the Blackstone Estate in Hackney. He was the oldest of six children. His parents were good people and both worked hard to make sure the children were well brought up. However, when Sunshine became a teenager he began to rebel and he and his friends got involved in minor crimes; shop lifting and vandalism. He was not academic and really struggled at school. At the age of fifteen he stopped going altogether. He got a job in Broadway market selling fruit and veg four days a week. But despite the support of his mum and dad he was slowly being sucked into a life of hanging around the streets and petty crime.

At the age of sixteen, his friend Keebles, persuaded him to try out a new gym that had just opened in Bethnal Green. It was a council initiative to get kids off the street and learn the disciplines associated with boxing. There he met Thomas Maligua who was in charge of the project. He became Sunshine's coach and eventually his friend. With Thomas' help he got to be a good boxer and was able to turn professional. He was not as good as he should have been, but still pretty decent. He didn't quite have the application, drive or willpower to get to the very top. What he did gain though was self-respect; he had finally found something he was really good at.

The more Sunshine Mawa thought about the beating he had taken, the angrier he became, especially as, weeks after, he was still feeling the pain. Whoever it was, owed him big time.

It had taken him another month to find the man who had delivered the worst beating he had ever received. He now knew his name was Justin McBride, and Sunshine's source had said he was a bloke not to be messed with, a real psychopath. Sunshine had laughed. He couldn't be that much of a tough guy with a name like Justin. However, the more he asked around the more uneasy he felt. Now he was in a quandary, should he just forget the whole thing; it was by far the safest option after all, or should he take a chance. Eventually his resentment grew to the point where he decided to take the risk. But he would use a softly softly approach and he would take precautions. He would have his girlfriend nearby, ready to call for help, if necessary.

He had discovered that McBride owned a house in New Cross in Southeast London. The ground floor was some kind of warehouse and upstairs were offices. The third floor was a large flat. Sunshine didn't think he lived there but seemed to go to the building pretty well every day.

This was the third day in a row that Sunshine and his girlfriend Lala had watched from an alleyway on the south side of the street. McBride always arrived between nine and half past and he and two others were dropped off outside. The driver would then drive off and come back and pick them up at lunchtime. Sunshine didn't stay after that, but he was confident that the two other men were his bodyguards.

"You stay here, baby girl. If Ise not out in a quarter of an hour, you calls the pol ees. You got it."

Lala shrugged.

"Yous sure yous understood?" said Sunshine.

Lala gave him an angry look and said in her south London accent. "Course I ave, I aint thick!"

Sunshine crossed the road and knocked. It was opened by a man in his fifties, wearing a light brown jacket, the type you often see worn by janitors or workers in warehouses.

"I'd like to speak to Mista McBride plees, I got some impotant busyness. My name is Sunshine Mawa. He know me."

The man walked over to a phone on the wall. Sunshine couldn't hear what was said.

"Follow me," he said.

They went up a flight of stairs and into an office. McBride was sitting behind a desk and Sunshine shuddered as he remembered the beating he had taken from this man. The two men he'd seen getting out of the car were standing near the window just behind him. On the floor, against the wall was a very large thick cardboard box. The room itself was dull, the walls a dirty green. There were no pictures or knick knacks anywhere, it was very sterile.

McBride rose and shook his hand in a friendly way. However, his eyes told a different story, they were dark and penetrating. Sunshine wasn't afraid of many people but this man gave him the creeps and a shiver went up and down his spine.

"Mr Mawa, what can I do for you?"

Standing there under McBride's scrutiny, Sunshine wished he was anywhere but where he was, but on the other hand, he was here now, he might as well do what he came for.

"Mista McBride, I don't wan to trouble you but after the beatin you give me, I was in da hospital for near five days and I still doesn't feels right. I wondered if you might just agree with me that it was worth a bit moa than the towzand pound you pays me."

McBride stared at him and then stood up and walked to the window.

"How much more do you think I should give you?"

"Maybe anoder two tousand, if dats awright."

"Ah, I wondered why you were keeping watch on my property these last few days, now I know."

McBride beckoned him over to the window.

"Take a look outside; do you notice anything Mr Mawa?"

Sunshine looked out and at first couldn't see anything different. Then he realised. Lala had gone, she wasn't where he had left her.

"My girlfriend gone. She were out dare," he said.

"That's right, she's gone to the same place you're going to."

At that moment the two men stepped forward and grabbed his arms in a tight grip. McBride took a plastic bag from his pocket and placed it over Sunshine's head and pulled the pull string at the bottom. Sunshine fought for all he was worth, but he was helpless, the two men were very strong and didn't give an inch.

As he weakened and the strength in his body ebbed away he was sure he could hear cheering in the distance and an image flashed through his mind. A boxer standing triumphant with his arms held aloft in victory.

THe world went black.

Chapter 7 The School Bully

The children had been with him just over a week when Daniel rang Shipham Primary School and made an appointment to see Mrs Parkin, the headteacher. She agreed to see him the following lunchtime. Daniel asked Jackie to meet him there, and when they all arrived, he left Ben and Lucy under the watchful eye of the school caretaker, Jodie Walsh. She took them to the nature room to see the animals and fish, one of the many amazing innovations that the school was well known for.

Mrs Parkin met them at the entrance of the school and led them to her office. Daniel estimated she was in her late forties and dressed fairly casually in slacks and a jumper, both brightly coloured. She definitely walked with a spring in her step.

On entering the headteacher's study, both Daniel and Jackie were surprised that the room did not look particularly impressive. The furniture was old and worn and the room could certainly do with a lick of paint.

"I know what you're thinking," said Mrs Parkin, "the truth is, we prefer to spend the money on things that directly benefit the children rather than posh offices. I actually prefer my office like this, it keeps my feet on the ground. Anyway, please sit down. How can I help you?"

Daniel and Jackie sat in chairs and Mrs Parkin sat with them, rather than behind her desk. Daniel was getting to really like this woman.

"Thanks for seeing us so quickly. I'm Daniel Pitt and this is my friend Jackie, here for moral support. My niece has had to go away for a while and has asked me to look after her children; a boy aged six and a girl aged nine. We live in the village; I am hoping you would be able to take them in for a short while, up to a term maximum?"

"I'm sure we can help with that. Give me the details of the school they usually go to and I'll sort it out."

"Right, that's where it gets difficult, unfortunately, I can't do that." said Daniel, "The problem is, my niece had to leave in a hurry and didn't give me that information, and I have no way of contacting her. Perhaps they could attend off the record as it's a short stay."

"I'm sorry Mr Pitt, you will have to contact your niece. We are not permitted to take new children without verifying their attendance at their previous school." She thought for a few seconds. "Surely if one of the children is nine, she would be able to give us the information we need; just the name of the school would do."

Daniel looked over to Jackie who gave a slight nod of the head, it was not missed by Mrs Parkin.

"Look, their attendance here can't be official, there really mustn't be any paperwork."

"Mr Pitt, I'm sorry, I don't know what is going on here but I can't take the children into the school without records, or, at the very least having contacted the previous school. I think you probably ought to go."

"Look, I don't know you personally but I was a governor here years ago and taught in Wells for over twelve years. The children will only be here for a short time, a term at most. I would be very grateful if you would trust me on this and bend the rules; there can be no record of them being here, none at all."

"I'm sorry, there are all sorts of regulations I have no choice but to abide by. I cannot ignore the rules."

She stood up and indicated that they should follow her to the door.

Daniel turned to Jackie. "I tried."

Jackie held out her warrant card, "Mrs Parkin, I am Detective Inspector Jackie Wentworth, based in Taunton. Are your staff trustworthy, could you trust them with confidential information."

"Yes, yes of course."

Jackie thought for a moment. "How many staff do you have, permanent staff that is, teachers and others?"

"Eleven in all."

"Please fetch them."

"I can't do that, some of them are on duty."

"It's lunchtime, I'm sure your lunchtime supervisors will cope for a few minutes. Go and fetch them, please. Otherwise, I will have to plant drugs in your desk drawer and arrest you for possession of drugs and a rickety desk."

The humour was lost on Mrs Parkin and she glared at Jackie and then walked out.

"That was a bit risky wasn't it?"

"No, I thought she was a good sort and would appreciate a bit of intelligent humour. Mind you, I have, on occasions, been known to be wrong.

"Are you going to tell them the truth?" asked Daniel.

"Part of it, certainly. I don't think there's a choice. If I was looking for children, the very first thing I would do is check for any new enrolments in schools, believe me it's not that difficult. We have to make absolutely sure there is no paperwork."

Mrs Parkin returned with nine others: six teachers, one school secretary and two classroom assistants. There was not a great deal of room but they managed to squeeze in.

"Two are on courses today, out of school; Mr Jones and Miss Gosling," said Mrs Parkin. "Everybody, this is Detective Inspector Wentworth and Mr Pitt. They want us to take two new pupils in rather unusual circumstances."

She indicated for Jackie to take over.

"I am going to give you the bare bones but I promise you that when this is all over I will return and tell you the full story. I also want you to know that I am not going to exaggerate in anything I am about to say. We want Ben and Lucy Hempleman to attend your school for the next term, maybe less than that. Those are not their real names. There must be no records of them having enrolled, nor of them attending the school. The reason is simple. It is quite likely that school documents would be accessed by criminals and if they then discovered the whereabouts of Ben and Lucy, the children would almost certainly be in great danger of being abducted and mistreated appallingly, and Daniel and possibly others would be in serious danger as well. There you have it. I plead with you that not one word of what I have just said leaves this room. Is that clear?"

"Is there nothing more you are able to tell us?" asked Mrs Parkin, obviously shocked by what she had just heard.

Jackie shook her head. "I'm afraid not."

Mrs Parkin looked at her staff carefully and then asked if Daniel and Jackie would step outside for a few minutes. Once they had gone she asked them all how they felt about what they were being asked to do. She felt very proud of her team as every one of them was in favour of taking the children as they were obviously 'in a bit of a pickle' as Mrs Sloan, the school secretary put it. Daniel and Jackie were called back into the room.

"Very well, we are all in agreement that we will take Ben and Lucy under the terms you have set out," Mrs Parkin said. "When you're gone, I will talk to everyone and sort out how we do this. Tomorrow I'll speak to Mr Jones and Miss Gosling; Ben will probably be in her class. One last thing though. Are my staff and pupils at risk of harm? Because if they are, my answer will certainly be no."

"Absolutely not," Jackie said, "there are only three ways that the children's whereabouts could be discovered, school records, by phone or by word of mouth. If you don't tell anyone, everything will be fine and if you do receive an inquiry asking if you have new pupils, you simply say no and contact Mr Pitt or me immediately, here's my card. I'm sure everything will be fine.

"OK, do any of you have any questions?" Everyone indicated that they didn't. "Very well, thanks everyone, I am sorry I interrupted your lunch break."

The staff filed out, all of them wishing they had been told more, it sounded intriguing.

"I am opening myself to possibly losing my career by doing this, in fact if someone was hurt because of me allowing these two children to attend without the proper authorisation, I could go to prison," Mrs Parkin said, once the others had gone and she had shut the door.

"First thing in the morning I will fax you a document, which will clearly state that I take full responsibility." Jackie replied.

"Very well." Mrs Parkin said, a little relieved but at the same time wondering if, in reality, the document would have any worth.

Daniel and Jackie thanked her and left.

Once outside, Jackie could see that Daniel was not at ease with what had just taken place. She waited patiently for him to get it off his chest.

"I hope we've done the right thing."

"Look, they have to go to school, otherwise people will talk or ring social services or something. I just hope I frightened them enough for them to keep their collective mouths shut."

"I don't know, they are bound to tell someone, it's human nature, it's a good piece of gossip."

"Even if they do," Jackie said, "how could it get back to McBride?"

"Is the document you're going to send her legal, I mean do you have the power to do that?"

"No, it will come from me, my bosses won't know about it, if it all goes pear shaped, I would be stuffed and probably so would she."

Daniel walked down to the school with the children at eight forty five the following Monday. Ben held Daniel's hand tightly and was obviously quite nervous. Lucy didn't seem worried at all.

When they got to the entrance, Daniel asked if they wanted him to go in with them. Before Ben could answer, Lucy grabbed hold of Ben's hand and marched him in. She told Daniel that she would look after him. Daniel watched until they were out of sight and went home.

Ben and Lucy's first few days at school were relatively uneventful. The teachers seemed kind and the other kids pretty much ignored them. Ben spent his break times watching the football match that took place in the playground every day. Most of the boys playing were a couple of years older than him and he noticed that one particular boy seemed to be in charge. He was bigger than the others and was a fierce tackler. They chose the teams using picks. The two captains took it in turns to choose a player.

On his fourth day, Ben plucked up courage and asked the boy in charge if he could join in. The boy turned and looked him up and down.

"No. Fuck off, you're too young and stupid."

He returned to the game.

A few minutes later the ball went off the imaginary pitch and fell at Ben's feet. He dribbled it a few yards and then kicked it back into play. The boss boy ran over and, without any warning pushed Ben to the floor.

"I told you, you couldn't play, you little weasel."

Lucy came from nowhere. She kicked him in the groin and then punched him in the head. The boy fell to the floor like a sack of potatoes. Lucy kicked him twice more in the ribs. All the footballers had seen what had happened and were standing looking in disbelief. Lucy turned and glared at them. They reluctantly turned away and carried on with the game.

"You can join in now," she said loudly. Ben looked a bit unsure. "Go on, join in," she ordered.

Ben joined the game and nobody objected.

Lucy turned to her victim, still lying on the ground and moaning. "What's your name?"

"Dennis." He replied meekly, still in a lot of pain.

She gently helped him to his feet and led him to a bench where they both sat down.

"Are you alright Dennis?" she said in a soothing tone.

"Suppose." He said and started crying. Where she had punched and kicked him hurt a lot but the fact he had been beaten up by a girl in front of his friends, was really painful and humiliating.

"Good," said Lucy, she turned towards him and looked him in the eyes and spoke in a quiet voice, "cos I want you to know something, and you need to listen very carefully cos it's important. Look at me Dennis. If you report me or tell anyone about this, I will break both your legs and kill your mother. And I really mean it. Do you understand what I'm saying?"

He nodded, stood up and hurried away.

That evening at tea there was a very uncomfortable and tense atmosphere. Suddenly Ben blurted out.

"I'm sorry, Lucy, I told Daniel what happened."

"You little squealer," she said with venom, staring at him.

"He's not a squealer, he was just telling me about his day, that's all." said Daniel.

"He is a squealer and anyway that boy started it, he beat up Ben." said Lucy angrily.

"No, he didn't beat up Ben; he pushed Ben," said Daniel quietly, "there's a massive difference. Look Lucy, whatever the rights and wrongs of what happened were, the real point is we don't want people gossiping about us. Suppose he tells on you?"

"He won't," said Lucy quickly with a slight smirk.

Daniel looked at her and a shiver went down his spine as he thought about the implications of what he had just heard. He had to decide quickly how to handle this, he knew telling her off wouldn't work.

"Alright, I know you want to protect your brother. Let's make a deal. How about you agree to warn people first and only turn to extreme violence as a last resort."

Despite herself, Lucy smiled. Daniel went to pat her on the shoulder but she immediately shrugged him off.

"Don't touch me," she said and walked out of the room.

Two weeks went by and, in his mind, Daniel reviewed how things were going. Ben was doing fine. He liked school and was quite relaxed and enjoying his life. Lucy however, had not made any friends at school; the other children were quite wary of her, for obvious reasons. She made sure she kept her distance from everyone she met, apart from Ben and never let Daniel get too close or enter her emotional world. She wouldn't even talk about school or friends. Daniel got all his information from Ben and occasional calls to the school. However, there were far less temper tantrums and she did seem to be a little more relaxed at home. The key was Harry. Both the kids loved the dog and he was, without doubt, a calming influence on Lucy. He gave her love and attention and asked for nothing in return.

Chapter 8 Barry

Although he didn't know it at the time, Barry Payne could not have had a worse start to life. As a toddler he regularly watched his father beat his mum senseless, usually as a result of her complaining that he had gambled away all her housekeeping money, which he did, regularly. Then, when he was four, after a drinking bout, his father, for no apparent reason, came home one night with a gun. He walked into the kitchen, aimed at her head and shot her dead, he then put the barrel in his mouth and fired. Barry was not found for forty eight hours.

For the next fifteen years he spent his childhood in care homes and with foster parents. He was not a violent boy but could be difficult at times and stubborn. He had horrible nightmares and regularly woke up screaming with anguish in the middle of the night. He never received treatment or counselling for the awful things he had witnessed as a child.

His last foster placement, when he was fourteen, was with George and Agnes Denby, who lived in Brockley, South London. George was a car mechanic by trade but in reality he made his money by servicing the cars of south London crooks and altering the appearance of stolen vehicles. They were lovely people and looked after Barry with a lot of love and understanding. With their help his nightmares became less frequent and finally stopped altogether.

George taught him how to drive; they would go down to a large supermarket car park in Weston Super Mare late at night and, before too long, Barry was proficient. He passed his test soon after his seventeenth birthday and loved driving in the countryside at high speeds.

Included on George's list of clients was a local gang boss called Justin McBride. George looked after and serviced all his vehicles. When McBride told him he was looking for a driver, someone who would be loyal, could drive fast but safely and could keep his mouth shut, George didn't hesitate before suggesting Barry.

And so, Barry became McBride's driver and was teamed up with Pamment and Fenton for particular jobs. To begin with he had no idea what kind of business they were really in. When he found out he was pretty sure that George and Agnes didn't know either.

All through his life, Barry avoided trouble and violence wherever he could. He was truly shocked and sickened by some of the things that he saw being done to the victims; those who had failed to pay their dues or had, in some way, upset or insulted the Boss, as McBride was called.

In order to cope he made a decision that he was employed as a driver and he would have nothing to do with the other things that happened; leave them to the other men. They all seemed to enjoy their work. In reality, he would like to have left, but he didn't really think that was an option, he was scared of what the consequences would be for him and George.

One morning Barry was called into McBride's office. By then he had been working for him just under a year. McBride walked round his desk and stood in front of Barry and without any warning punched him hard in the stomach. Barry fell to the floor, gasping for breath.

McBride looked down at him and said, "Do you know why I did that Barry?"

Barry tried to think of anything he had done wrong.

"No boss."

McBride stared down at him for what seemed a long time but was probably less than a minute. Then, seemingly satisfied, he said.

"Because I can. Now get up and sit on that chair."

He continued to stare at Barry; eyes almost black and hooded, staring out of a face, half hidden in shadow, that reminded Barry of something out of a horror movie. Barry was very frightened and couldn't really work out what was happening. Finally, McBride looked away and spoke gently.

"Do you know, Barry, I think you are the type of person I can trust? You're not a killer, I know that, in fact I don't think you like the violence you see regularly working here. That's why I've supported you when Pamment moans about you not helping them with the dirty work. I've told him; you're the driver, bottom line. So, Barry I am going to trust you with a very important task and you're not going to breathe a word about it to anyone else, ever, clear?"

"Yes boss."

"If you let me down by blabbing to anyone, even your teddy bear, while I'm alive, or by failing to carry out the task when I'm dead, you will not believe the pain and horror that will rain down on you. Clear?"

"Yes Boss."

McBride passed over a piece of paper with a number written on it. "That is the combination to open the wall safe over there, memorise it and then burn it.

Now, If I were to die, which I'm well aware can happen at any time in my line of work, I want you to open the safe and inside you'll find a large package and a load of cash. I want you to take the package and deliver it to a firm of solicitors in the Strand. They're called Telfer, Lilley and Hebden. Say it's from Mr McBride, they'll know exactly what to do with it. Oh, and you can keep the cash. It's yours. Got it?"

"Yes Boss."

"You see Barry, of all the people who work for me, you are the only one I actually trust. Now get out."

Barry learnt to live with his misgivings and just tried to close his mind to the violence he saw every day. It just about worked for him.

But then they did the one thing he couldn't ignore or forgive; they killed Kim. One day she would have justice. One day.

He had always hated the way McBride treated his children, they often went hungry and were ignored. He hit them if they were slow to follow an instruction and he did not allow the things that normal kids took for granted; birthdays, Christmas presents, firework night, even eating normally as a family. How could someone treat children like that, especially when they were their own?

He never saw McBride hit Kim but he knew he did, he saw the bruises and the other men told him.

Whenever the opportunity presented itself and McBride was not about, he would try to chat to Kim in a normal way. It was difficult as she was often drunk. He also brought sweets and bits of food for Zeta and Eddie but always made sure they knew not to mention it to their dad.

He knew that he was the nearest thing Kim had to a friend. Yet, he had stood by and let Pamment and Fenton kill her on McBride's orders. He'd sat in the car like the coward he was and had done nothing. When he got home that evening he had started sobbing, ignored George and Agnes and went straight to his room and threw himself on his bed. George and Agnes entered his room and Agnes took him into her arms and George gently asked him what was wrong. He told them everything that had happened; the killings, the beatings, the way the children were treated and the death of Kim.

"I could have stopped them and saved her, I'm a complete coward, I'm just as bad as they are."

"No son, you couldn't and you're not," said George, "if you had tried to intervene they would have killed you as well and, if you had got away, they would have hunted you down and probably murdered Agnes and me as a warning to others. You did the only thing you could. Now try to get some sleep and in the morning you go to work and act as if everything's fine."

Agnes and George were totally shocked by what they had heard, they had no idea what kind of a man they had persuaded Barry to work for. All they could do was agree to support him the best they could.

Chapter 9 Lions, bikes and a handshake

Daniel Pitt was not a rich man. He had his pension and he had accrued savings over the years. He didn't drink a great deal or smoke, rarely went on holiday and when he did it was in the UK and accompanied by Harry.

His wife, Mary, had been left nearly three hundred thousand pounds when her mother died. That had all been put away and, when the time came, Daniel was able to help his three children buy their first homes. When they had moved in, he had visited each of them and taken a beautiful, framed painting of Mary so they could hang it somewhere prominent and always remember her.

So, when he decided to organise a two night break for Ben and Lucy at Centre Parks in Wiltshire, he knew it would not break the bank. What he hoped it would do, was give them a great time, relax them and, hopefully, help show Lucy that not all men were evil. His great ambition was that he could bond with Lucy.

A lady down the road took in people's dogs and didn't charge too much. Harry had been there before a few times and had always eagerly run into her house. Daniel dropped him off the following Monday. The kids had no idea where they were going when they set off around nine thirty; they were very excited. They had never been on holiday before. Daniel knew that their cabin in Centre Parks would not be ready until mid-afternoon, so he drove to the nearby Longleat safari park, where he had booked a tour in a jeep for just the three of them.

They had a wonderful time, driving very close to the famous Longleat lions and had the driver, who doubled as a guide, laughing when Lucy tried to persuade Ben to get out of the jeep and stroke on of them. They saw giraffes, zebras and rhinos from the jeep and were allowed out to approach a huge camel. Lucy stroked his nose and fed him some stuff that looked like crushed peanuts. Ben watched from a few feet away but wouldn't go any closer. As they drove away Lucy turned to Daniel.

"He was a bit smelly, that camel, I can still smell it on my clothes."

"That's a coincidence, because the camel said the same about you," replied Daniel.

For a second Lucy laughed and Daniel thought she was going to playfully push him, but she remembered in time and turned away. Daniel was disappointed, but she was enjoying herself and that was progress.

They moved into their cabin and unpacked their bags and then Daniel told them he had another surprise for them. He took them to a large building, opened the door and there was a huge heated indoor swimming pool, with slides, toys and balls to play on and with. Lots of children were there enjoying the water. He handed Lucy a blue swimming costume and Ben a pair of red trunks that he had bought specially. He pointed them in the direction of the changing rooms. He was surprised by their reaction, they just stood there looking at the water. Finally, Lucy spoke.

"I'm not going in there," and she threw her costume to the floor.

"I don't want to either," said Ben.

"But it's a swimming pool, don't you like to swim?"

"We've never been swimming," said Ben.

"Would you not like to play in the shallow bits?"

"Oh, yae, great," said Lucy, "and have all those wankers laugh at us, bollocks to that."

Without waiting for Daniel to reply, she walked out.

Later, they picked up fish and chips and ate in the cabin. Daniel asked them if they wanted to play cards, which they did for a while, but Lucy got bored and said she was going to bed to read. Ben followed soon afterwards, Daniel felt very deflated and fed up.

In bed Daniel thought about the day; the safari park had been a great success but it had been negated by the swimming fiasco; in hindsight he should have asked them first. He was on a real learning curve.

He thought about his plans for the next day. He'd booked a boat trip on the lake to see the seals, followed by a drive through the monkey enclosure. He'd also booked cycle hire in the afternoon and they'd go for a ride in the forest; apparently there were loads of cycle tracks. In the evening, he had reserved a table at the site restaurant and the kids could have pizza if they wanted. Daniel had brought some board games, so they could play Topple or Snakes and Ladders before bed. He could see no flaw in his plans.

The boat trip went down really well. The silly seals, as Ben called them, were hilarious and followed the boat, leaping out of the water. They put on a great performance. They also saw some hippos which they hadn't expected. Daniel was really surprised when the boatman told them that hippos can't swim and you only ever find them in shallow water, however, they are able to hold their breath for as long as six minutes. Lucy suggested that they should hold Ben underwater for six minutes to see if he was a hippo. Ben paid her back by sticking his tongue out at her.

At the monkey enclosure they were in a line of cars waiting to enter. Daniel was a little perturbed by a big sign which read-

WARNING

The monkeys may damage your car

Drivers enter at their own risk

Some people were leaving the queue and heading out. Daniel decided it was worth the risk. The convoy moved slowly through and it wasn't long before they saw their first monkey. It was great fun and both Lucy and Ben were soon laughing at the antics of the animals.

Suddenly, Ben shouted, "Daniel look!"

A monkey was hanging off the roof rack on the back of the car in front and was literally ripping off the rear windscreen wiper. Lucy started laughing as did Ben. Daniel thought it was quite amusing as well, as long as it was somebody else it was happening to. The car stopped and the driver opened his door but closed it hurriedly when he saw three monkeys charging towards him. At that moment a safari jeep pulled up and a warden got out and shooed the offending monkey away. The driver wound down his window and, looking very cross, said something. The warden just shrugged and drove off.

While eating their cheese and pickle sandwiches at lunchtime, Ben and Lucy talked about their morning with great enthusiasm. 'Success,' thought Daniel.

When the children were introduced to their hire bikes, Daniel could see straight away there was a problem. Ben looked worried and Lucy looked at the bike and was obviously feeling cross.

"Oh God," said Daniel, "you've never ridden a bike before, have you? Look it's easy, I'll show you then you can have a go. If you don't like it we'll do something else."

Daniel got on his bike and pedalled up the path and back. He then helped Ben on to his. Lucy refused any help and mounted hers. Daniel encouraged them to take their foot off the ground and pedal. As soon as Lucy started peddling she fell sideways onto the tarmac. Daniel let go of Ben to try to help and Ben fell over too.

A family comprising of mum, dad and a boy of about twelve, who were just returning their bikes, were nearby, and both the father and son started laughing.

"What a pair of losers," said the boy.

Before Daniel could stop her, Lucy got up and charged at the boy. She knocked him to the ground, sat astride of him and raised her fist with intention of punching him in the face. Daniel managed to get there first.

"No Lucy, NO!"

Lucy looked at Daniel then at the boy, spat at him in the face, got off him and walked away.

The father charged up to Daniel.

"That girl's a bloody maniac, you should have her on a lead."

"Well perhaps you should set a better example to your son and not laugh when someone else is struggling, and maybe even tell him off for making unkind and derogatory remarks."

"Well, you're their dad, perhaps you should have bloody well taught them to ride a bike at their age."

Daniel was furious, he grabbed hold of the man's arm and dragged him away so they could not be overheard.

"Stop behaving like a cretin and listen to me," he said in a quiet voice. "I am not their father. Their father didn't teach them to ride bikes or anything else. The only thing he taught them was violence and hatred, and you should be fucking ashamed of yourself for the way you and your son are behaving. You cannot begin to imagine what those two have been through."

Daniel stared at him, he knew he was very close to losing it, and putting this moron in hospital and, at that moment, he really didn't care. A lot depended on what happened next.

"I'm really sorry, I didn't know, but you're right, we shouldn't have laughed anyway. I'll talk to Colin." He said after thinking for a few seconds.

He held out his hand, Daniel looked round and saw that everyone was watching him. He decided he should show a good example to the children and shook hands. The man walked up to Ben and Lucy and said sorry to them as well.

They left the bikes where they were and went for a walk up Cley Hill instead, which was nearby. They played hide and seek, and, when Ben was hiding, Lucy tried to persuade Daniel to leave him and go back to the chalet. He hoped she was joking. Anyway, they had a good time and soon forgot the bike incident.

The following morning, they stayed in Centre Parcs and did some of the available activities there: table tennis, snooker, ten pin bowling and darts. The first time Ben actually got a dart to land on the board, earned him a cheer from lots of people in the room. It was good natured and Ben smiled shyly. Daniel tried hard to engineer Ben winning at something but failed, Lucy was having none of it. To be fair, Ben didn't seem to mind too much. After lunch they headed home.

That evening, the children were sitting on the sofa in their pyjamas waiting for Daniel to bring their pre-bed milk and biscuit. As he walked in the sitting room they were talking quietly. Daniel thought immediately that they were up to something. After they had finished their supper, they walked over to him, he felt a little nervous, they were children of habit, this was not normal.

"Daniel," said Ben, trying to be grown up but actually looking very emotional, "Thank you for taking us to Centre Parcs. We think it was the best thing that's ever happened."

He gave Daniel a hug leaving snot on his jumper and then walked away.

Lucy stepped forward.

"Thank you," she said. "It was great."

She put her hand out. They shook hands.

"And thanks for sticking up for us with that man and his twat of a son."

She looked embarrassed, turned and pushed Ben out of the door and they both went to bed.

Daniel felt quite emotional and was struggling not to cry. Shaking hands had been the first time he had had any physical contact with Lucy. He wanted so much to take her in his arms and cuddle her, but in his heart, he knew it was the wrong thing to do. Small steps.

Chapter 10 McBride

Justin Edwin Montgomery McBride was born to a wealthy family and was the second of three boys. They were brought up by their mother whose sole job was the running of the house and bringing up the children. His father was an importer and exporter, mainly of wine, spirits and cigarettes.

He had set up his business during the second world war and had made his first ten thousand pounds through sales on the black market. However, his business now was almost totally legitimate and lawful. He didn't quite pay the full amount of tax that he probably should have done but, in his mind, that was just part of the game. He had very little to do with the bringing up of his children and rarely spent any time with them.

They lived, deep in the countryside, in a large six bedroom house, or mansion some would say, in Chobham, Surrey, just a ten minute walk from the famous treacle mine on Chobham Clump. Two full time gardeners looked after their extensive grounds and a cleaner was employed for twelve hours a week to keep the house spick and span. In the wide driveway at the front of the house were their two jaguars that were replaced for new each year.

Mrs McBride began to worry about Justin at a very early age. He often displayed signs of violence in the games he played, firstly with his little brother and by the time he was seven he had complete dominion over his older brother of nine as well; he had beaten him up several times. His two brothers avoided any contact with him whenever they could. Mrs McBride was for ever telling little Justin off.

He was sent home regularly from his local school for fighting and once punched a girl so hard, she had to go to hospital. The crunch came when he threw a chair at a teacher and then tried to punch and kick her. He was sent home and his parents were told in no uncertain terms that he would not be welcome back.

The adult McBrides decided the only answer was to send him to a private school, where he would get a bit of discipline and be whipped into shape, as Mr McBride put it. He was enrolled at the Winston Churchill Academy for boys in Weymouth, where he boarded during the term. They didn't receive any complaints so they assumed everything was going well at school. However, the whole family dreaded it when he came home for the holidays.

At the end of the academic year, they got a shock; a letter arrived from the school saying that Justin would not be allowed back after the holidays. They tried hard to find out why, but all the school would say was that his behaviour was unbecoming of a pupil at the academy.

After some research they managed to find a school in Bristol that took a lot of foreign students. They were more than happy for the students to remain at the school in the holidays for the right financial settlement. He lasted sixteen months.

In the following years he attended three more establishments and was expelled from each of them, the last one within four days. At that point his father decided enough was enough. By then Justin was sixteen. Mr McBride offered him a deal. He would give him one hundred thousand pounds if he left home and never came back. Typically, despite it being an enormous amount of money, Justin said no; with a smirk he said he liked being with his mummy and daddy and his two lovely brothers too much to think of leaving.

However, eventually, and after a great deal of negotiation, he accepted a payment of a quarter of a million pounds. He packed a bag, walked out of the door, got into one of the Jaguars and drove away. The Jaguar had not been part of the deal nor did Justin have a license, but his father and mother really didn't care. The relief they felt was well worth the cost. No-one in the family ever saw Justin again and they were not in the least bit sorry.

McBride arrived in London and bought a building in New Cross. The ground floor was a storage area, the first floor offices and the second floor was an apartment which was, and remained, his official home, although later he bought a second house in Blackheath overlooking the heath itself. This was where he eventually lived. Having settled in, he began to find out as much as he could about the area in which he lived. He frequented pubs and clubs around New Cross and Deptford to ascertain who the crime bosses were. It turned out there was only one, Ralph Chase. He collected protection money from shops and businesses and ran prostitution and the drugs trade in Deptford, New Cross and on down the Old Kent Road as far as the border with Peckham.

For two months McBride tried to meet him. Finally, he sent a very expensive watch to Chase and managed to get an appointment. They met at Chase's night club in Deptford an hour or so before it was due to open. McBride was searched and then shown into an office. Chase was smoking a cigar and was sitting behind a large desk. He had three bodyguards with him.

"You've got five minutes," said Chase.

McBride replied, "Thank you for seeing me Mr Chase, I've heard a lot about you and you are obviously a man who deserves respect. I would like to work for you. I am tough, strong and have no worries about hurting people when required. I could collect debts, work in one of your clubs or be your enforcer, if you needed one."

"How old are you, young man?"

"Nearly seventeen sir."

"Well son," said Chase, "come back in a few years, I ain't needing an enforcer at the moment and I'm good for muscle." He nodded and signalled for McBride to be shown out.

McBride had expected this, the main thing was that he'd got his name out there. Chase knew who he was. Actually, as he was about to leave, he had a really lucky break. When walking down the corridor towards the exit of the club, he heard a man behind him.

"Oy, McBride, I want a word with you! I'm Bennie, I gather you're after taking my job. Well, I am Mr Chase's enforcer and I just want you to know that I never want to see you again, you fucking little pusspot. Got it?"

He punched McBride in the stomach, who sank to the ground, gasping for breath.

"Next time I see you, I'll knock every tooth out of that big fat mouth of yours, you cocky little bastard." He stamped on McBride's chest and walked away.

Two weeks later McBride turned up at the same club and asked to see Mr Chase, he said it was urgent. The bouncer made a call and told him Mr Chase wasn't interested.

"It's really urgent and Mr Chase will want to hear what I have to say. Please give him this envelope. He will be really angry if you don't."

The bouncer looked at his colleague who nodded and he walked into the club. Five minutes later he returned and signalled McBride to follow him. He entered the same office as before with the same bodyguards looking as fierce as ever. Chase was sitting behind his desk, in front of him was the envelope and lying next to it was a severed thumb. McBride took out another envelope and placed it near the first one. Chase signalled to one of his men who searched McBride and shook his head.

Chase pointed at the thumb. "What the fuck is this?"

McBride picked up the other envelope and emptied it onto the desk. Four fingers tumbled out.

"I apologise for this, Mr Chase, I'm aware that I'm being a bit dramatic but, when I left you last time, I was accosted by your enforcer, Bennie, he should be called 'not worth a penny'. He punched me in the stomach and stamped on me, causing me considerable pain, and threatened to kill me. He treated me with no respect whatsoever. I'm sure you understand I could not let that go. So, one night I followed him to his flat, overpowered him and tied him to a chair.

"Mr Chase, you would have been ashamed of him, he cried like a baby and begged for mercy as I cut off his fingers. It was embarrassing. In fact, he was so noisy I had to tape his mouth closed. In the end I finished him off to put him out of his misery. Oh, and please don't worry, no one will ever find his body.

"So, I think you have a vacancy for an enforcer, Mr Chase, and I would like to apply. It would be an honour to serve you and I would be happy to do anything that you ask of me. You would have my total loyalty. Oh, and by the way, I'm now seventeen."

The enforcer, Bennie, was the first man that McBride had killed and, thinking about it later, he realised, it was one of the best experiences he had ever had.

Chapter 11 The Theft

One Friday, Daniel was thinking about where he could take the children over the weekend. He had a look at the Mendip Times to see what was going on in the area and found that the following day, Saturday the tenth of December, the Christmas market was taking place in Axbridge. On the first Saturday of the month there was always a local produce market in Axbridge, a few miles from Shipham, but as it was Christmas they were holding it on the second Saturday for some reason that was lost in the annals of time. Daniel decided to take the children and let them have a wander round and get a feel for rural life.

The next day they set off and on the way he told them about Cheddar Man.

"Axbridge is a really old town that's always had a market once a month. On the edge of the square is a museum. It's really interesting and free, run by volunteers. I'll take you there sometime. Anyway, in one of the rooms, there are the remains of Cheddar Man who was found in a cave. The cave was discovered by a chap called Gough in Cheddar Gorge in 1903 and believe it or not, is ten thousand years old. Do you know what DNA is?"

"No," said Ben.

"I do," said Lucy, "if you committed a crime, Ben, you might leave behind DNA in your blood or sweat or even your skin. Everybody's different so they can tell it's you who done it."

Daniel was really impressed. He looked at her in the mirror. "You are very knowledgeable, Lucy."

Lucy looked away but he noticed there was a hint of a smile.

"Anyway," continued Daniel, "They can also tell if you're related to someone through DNA. They managed to get DNA from Cheddar Man, they actually extracted it from the inside of one of his molar teeth, which I think is really remarkable that it should last all that time. Anyway, they invited anyone whose family had lived in the area from way back, to come and be tested to see if they were related to Cheddar man. Incredibly they got a DNA match. Of all the people it could have been, he turned out to be a history teacher at the Kings of Wessex secondary school, a chap called Adrian Target. He was a direct descendant of Cheddar Man from ten thousand years ago. Fantastic eh?"

Nobody answered, Daniel wasn't sure if they weren't impressed, didn't understand, or perhaps just didn't feel the need to comment.

When they arrived at the market, he explained that there were lots of different foods on sale as well as jewellery, pottery, toys, soaps and other stuff. All of it was made or grown locally. He gave each of them a pound and pointed to the bread stall and told them to meet him there in an hour.

"Keep together, Lucy, don't let Ben out of your sight."

Daniel wandered off to get a coffee hoping that giving them a bit of freedom would help them trust him more, especially Lucy.

Lucy waited until Daniel had gone into the café at the side of the square and then she spoke quietly to Ben for a few minutes and took his pound. She wandered over to the jewellery stall. The jeweller greeted her with a smile. He certainly knew how to advertise his products, he had a stud in both his ear and his nose, a necklace with a green stone hanging and a ring on every finger. Lucy approached him picked up a ring and studied it.

"OK if I try this on?" she said.

"Sure, have you got some money or are you just having a look?"

Lucy showed him the two pounds and moved to the side of stall pretending she could see the ring more clearly in the weak sunshine. The stall holder was watching her carefully. Meanwhile, Ben, very quietly, approached the stall from the other side and took a pair of cufflinks which he slipped into his pocket and walked away.

"How much?" Lucy asked.

"Four pound fifty," said the stall holder, "it's silver and the stone is aquamarine."

"I've only got two pounds. Would you take that?"

"Sorry love, cost me more than that to make it."

Lucy returned the ring, thanked the man and then walked away to join Ben.

Next, Lucy approached a young man and asked in her 'butter wouldn't melt in my mouth' way if she could have one of his carrier bags. He obliged with a smile. She gave the bag to Ben and they approached the fruit and veg stall. Ben asked for a paper bag and surreptitiously tore the bottom. Holding the paper bag above the plastic bag he took ten apples and dropped five of them in, allowing them to drop down into the plastic bag. Lucy was keeping the stall holder busy by asking what the various unusual looking vegetables were. Ben then asked for a new bag as the other one was torn and, eventually, Lucy paid for just five apples.

Ten minutes later Daniel came out of the café and a man called Jed approached him and they shook hands.

"Hi Daniel, how are you doing?"

"Fine thanks Jed, you alright? Any murders or riots yet for you to deal with?"

Jed looked confused until Daniel pointed to Jed's badge with security printed on it.

"Oh, I see, no, nothing like that" said Jed, "but we have had a couple of robberies though. I've just watched a couple of kids steal a pair of cufflinks and some fruit; apples I think. A girl about nine or ten and a younger boy, who could have been her brother. I thought I saw them with you earlier."

"Oh, no." said Daniel, his heart sinking.

"Who are they Daniel, not your grandchildren are they?"

"They're my niece's kids, I'm looking after them for a few weeks. Will you let me sort this out Jed. Please?"

"OK, but probably best if you took them home afterwards."

"Thanks Jed, I owe you a pint."

Daniel walked over to the bread stall where the children were waiting.

"OK, a lot depends on what happens in the next few minutes. Firstly, give me whatever you stole from the jewellery stall."

Lucy and Ben looked at each other for a few seconds, then Lucy gave him a slight nod of the head. Ben took out the cufflinks and handed them to Daniel.

"Good, how many apples did you steal?"

Both children spoke at the same time, Ben said five and Lucy two.

"And how many did you pay for?"

Ben said five and Lucy eight. She glared at him.

"Maybe it was five." she muttered looking at the ground.

Daniel took five apples and the cufflinks and told the children to stay put. He walked over to where Jed was standing watching.

"Will you deal with these Jed; you know get them back to their owners. Sometime, I promise, I'll tell you what's going on but I can't now. It's vital these two don't attract any attention." Jed snorted. "Please, as a favour to me, just forget what happened here.... Two pints?"

"Go on then, I'm sure you've got your reasons; two pints it is."

He walked away towards the jewellery stall.

Daniel led Ben and Lucy around a corner to a small tearoom called The Almshouse.

"Why? Why did you do that?"

"The cufflinks were for you for Christmas," Lucy blurted out, anger in her voice.

Daniel was shocked. "Do you really think that I want a present for Christmas that you stole? Look, did you do this a lot in London? I suppose you thought that here in Somerset the local yokels would be too thick to catch you."

Ben said, "Sometimes when my mum was ill and couldn't get up, we had to steal. We didn't have anything to eat."

"We didn't have any money either. I had to look after Ben so we stole some food. So what? We was good at it. Anyway, she wasn't ill at all, he beat her up; either that or she was pissed."

"Would you be willing to tell the police that?" asked Daniel.

"No NO!" Lucy said aggressively, "anyway, some of the police were his friends. I saw him paying one once. I won't talk to the police and nor will Ben."

Ben started to cry, he clung to Lucy. The owner of the café, Meg, approached the table. She had a broad smile and gave every impression of being a warm, caring and motherly type of person.

"I'm Meg and I be thinking there only be one way to cure children when they be upset and crying and that's a nice piece of my best chocolate cake for each of them, baked this very morning from all the bestest of ingredients. He'll take the tears away." She put the plates down in front of them. "There you go my lovelies."

Daniel picked up his wallet and took out a five pound note.

"No, no need for that, it's a gift from me to these sweet little things."

Lucy muttered a thankyou but Ben got up and wrapped his arms round her, burying himself in her apron. She winked at Daniel and wandered back to the counter.

"Why did she do that?" asked Lucy.

"I don't know, she's just a kind person I guess."

Lucy thought for a few seconds. "People are a bit nice round here."

"Yes, most are. And they're ordinary. The people you stole from this morning, they're not rich, they're just working people trying to make a living and afford a nice Christmas with their families. The last thing they need is people stealing from them."

"Will you send us away?" asked Ben, still sobbing.

"I want you to promise, no more stealing or doing anything else that attracts attention. If you want to stay with me, I need you to promise."

"We promise," said Lucy after a few seconds.

Daniel looked at them both.

"OK. No, of course I'm not going to send you away. Apart from anything else, I can't think of anyone else who would put up with two scallywags like you. We'd better get going. Harry hasn't been fed yet and that's why they call him Hungry Harry."

"I thought you said he was called Handsome Harry the Hunter." said Ben.

"Yes," said Daniel, "Handsome Harry the Hungry Hunter."

"Oh no, not this again!" said Lucy.

Ben started to laugh and soon they were all laughing.

They got up and then Lucy grabbed one of the apples and told Ben to come with her. They went up to Meg and gave her the apple. She was really touched and gave them both a hug.

"Bye Meg," they said.

"Laters, me dears." She replied.

On the way to the car Lucy mentioned that Meg had said some strange things.

"She called the piece of cake he, and afterwards, she said laters, I suppose that meant see you later."

"That's old Mendip speak," said Daniel, "the older people, who've lived in this part of Somerset all their lives still speak that way."

Lunch was a quiet affair and afterwards Ben went out to play with Harry. Harry, however, wasn't interested and crept upstairs. He pushed open Daniel's bedroom door with his nose and climbed onto the bed for a nap. Ben followed him up.

Daniel sat in the living room reading and Lucy was in an armchair staring out of the window. When the doorbell rang they both jumped slightly, pulled out of their own worlds.

"That'll be Jackie, let her in please and then go and find Ben and give him a hand harassing the dog, he's not as expert as you. I think they might be upstairs somewhere."

Lucy went up and found them both fast asleep on the bed. She joined them and snuggled up to Harry. He sighed contentedly and placed his paw across her tummy. Lucy smiled. Despite everything, she felt relaxed and the worry she constantly felt in the pit of her stomach had temporarily abated. She didn't often feel that way. She shut her eyes and slept peacefully.

Jackie came in and flopped onto a chair, she looked tired.

"You look tense, Daniel. Trouble?"

"Oh, nothing really. Within two minutes of being at school, Lucy kicked the shit out of the school bully. To be fair to her he had had the audacity to lay hands on her helpless little brother. On the plus side, if any adults saw it happen, they pretended they hadn't and I suspect Lucy dealt with the possibility of the aforementioned school bully reporting it. Then today I took them to Axbridge market and they robbed two stalls.

Jackie laughed, "I'm sorry Daniel, it's not funny, I know, but she is a bit of a lovable rogue."

"She's spent her life watching her mum getting beaten up, foraging for food and supporting Ben. Some of it must have rubbed off. I wouldn't want to be her enemy," said Daniel. "We did have a good time at Centre Parcs for a couple of days though. Few hairy moments but, on the whole, it went well.

"Well, you've had them a lot longer than we said. Do you want rid of them?"

Daniel thought for a few seconds. "No, truth is I quite enjoy having them here, they're good kids really. The dog likes them; he's a good judge of character. I'll keep them a bit longer."

"Underneath that, 'I hate kids,' you're a big softy really." laughed Jackie. "Well, Christmas coming up. Any plans. I see your decorations are up. Very tasteful. Did the kids help?"

"There's a fine line between help and hinder. My family are all coming down over Christmas. I think Ben and Lucy will enjoy that. I think my lot will as well. I'll have to tell them some of the truth. Do you want to join us?

"Nice offer but no, I have plans and I'm on duty Christmas Day."

"Cup of tea?" asked Daniel.

"No thanks, I've tasted your tea before!"

They sat in a comfortable silence for a while.

"What about you, Jackie, you never talk about yourself. Have you got a boyfriend since you divorced Robert?"

"No, but I do have a partner I live with, her name's Jenny."

"Oh my god, I'm so sorry, I just assumed ... that's great. Can I meet her some time?"

"Probably not."

"Shame really, I was going to offer to have a steamy but casual relationship with you, just for a few wonderful and fulfilling nights. Any chance of a threesome?"

Jackie laughed, "None whatsoever. Anyway, you're too old and believe me you wouldn't cope."

She stood up. "On that note I'd better go. See ya. Call me if you need me."

Daniel saw her out the front door and called out.

"How about a foursome, we could include Harry?"

Jackie stuck one finger up at him and then blew him a kiss. She got in her car and drove off, smiling.

When Jackie had gone, Daniel called the two children to come down. They came into the room looking very bleary eyed.

On the right of Daniel's front door there was a room that was always kept closed. It was to this that Daniel took them.

"Have either of you been in here?" asked Daniel.

Lucy shook her head.

"I opened the door once but it was dark, I walked in a little bit and a light suddenly came on. I was scared and went straight out, sorry Daniel if I did anything wrong," said Ben.

"No, it's OK Ben you didn't do anything. You are welcome to go into any room, except for one that's got a million pounds in it of course."

Daniel took them in and, at first, they couldn't see anything as the thick curtains were closed. They went further in and suddenly lights started flickering on against the wall to their left. Daniel flicked a switch and the main light came on and they were able to see sets of shelves. Each light was attached to the bottom of a shelf and lit what was on the shelf below when someone went near it. There were three units against the wall, each with four shelves that had labels on the front: Minerals, Rocks or Fossils. The display was stunning; each shelf was full of items; of all colours, shapes and sizes. Some of the fossils were huge. The children were amazed. They rushed over to look properly.

"Can we pick things up?" asked Ben.

"Sure, only pick up one thing at a time please and put it back where it came from. Every piece is labelled and some are in groups, like quartz. Quartz comes in all sorts of shapes and colours. There's also a group called metals and another which is all precious stones.

The children picked up lots of things and studied them and put them back carefully. They were very respectful. Daniel was always amazed at how interested they were whenever they were shown anything new. Ben picked up a huge slab of rock.

"This looks like a plant."

"It sort of is, it's a fern or the imprint of a fern. It's two hundred and fifty million years old."

"Wow," said Lucy, smiling, "that's even older than you Daniel. Did you find it?"

"Cheeky, yes, I got it from an old coal mine waste tip near Radstock. Not too far from here."

"Is this really a ruby?" asked Lucy.

"Yes, it's in rock, called its matrix. You can't make jewellery with it though, it's not good enough quality."

"Did you find everything?" asked Ben.

"A bit less than a half, I would say. Have you ever been to Covent Garden market."

"Yes," said Lucy, "mum sometimes took me on a Sunday. But then dad said we couldn't go anymore."

"Well, when I started teaching, I worked in London and I was always broke, never had enough money so I managed to rent a stall at Greenwich Market and then later at Covent Garden every Sunday. I sold minerals, fossils and jewellery to make some extra cash; I had three children to feed and they could all eat for England."

"Where did you live in London?" asked Lucy.

"In Penge, in southeast London. I actually went to university near where you lived in New Cross. Goldsmiths College, part of London University."

"Wow, I used to sneak in there sometimes," said Lucy, "They had a big thing called a refectory where everyone went to eat. I used to stand behind one of the pillars so the people who worked there couldn't see me. I'd ask the students if they would buy me a bun or a bottle of pop. A lot of them were really nice but then someone must have grassed me up and they watched out for me. I couldn't get in anymore."

"Well, if I'd seen you, I would most certainly have grassed you up. Come over here a minute."

He turned on another light and took them to the other side of the room where there was a table. On it were several cabinets made of wood, with small draws in them. He opened one of the draws.

"So, these bits are called findings and this is the ring drawer, necklaces and earrings in this one, broaches and tie pins in the bottom one; they're all silver. In these drawers are loads of different minerals that have been shaped and polished to go in the jewellery; they are called cabochons. That's tiger eye, opal; that's my favourite, opal. So, people would come to the stall and choose a finding and a cabochon and we would tell them to go round the market and come back in half an hour while we made the piece. They probably thought it was really skilful but actually, we just glued the cabochon on with super glue. Why don't you both make something you like.

"Now?" asked Lucy.

"Why not?"

Ben said, "boys don't wear jewellery."

"Well," said Daniel, "some boys do, but if you like, you could make your teacher something for Christmas. You can tell her you made it yourself."

Daniel got them to practise using a cheap finding and a carnelian cabochon of which he had hundreds. He then let them choose a silver finding and any cabochon they wanted. Ben chose a pendant and a lapis lazuli cabochon; Lucy chose a ring with opal.

"Trust you two to choose the most expensive things," said Daniel. "I wouldn't do a ring though Lucy if I were you, unless it's for you. You have to know the finger size. It would be alright if the person you were making it for was here, you could try it on them."

It always amazed Daniel, watching Lucy helping Ben, how gentle and patient she was. She was always insulting him which he never seemed to mind. Daniel was sure that Ben knew she loved him and would always be there for him. They made their items and left them on the table to set.

As they were leaving the room the children realised there were cabinets and shelves all-round the room and many paintings on the wall.

"They're good. Did you paint them?" asked Lucy.

"Yes but don't be fooled. For every decent painting I did, there were loads of rubbish ones that ended up in the bin."

"Can we come in here on our own and look at stuff?" asked Lucy.

"Any time you like."

"Are there any drawers you don't want us to look in?"

"No, you can look in what you like. I trust you. The only thing I ask is that your careful and put things back as they were. And if you do have an accident, tell me, don't try to hide it. I won't be cross. Well, unless it's Ben, then I might have to cut his head off and add it to my animal and human head collection.

"I wonder which section Ben would be in," said Lucy with a smile.

Ben made a face at her and Daniel managed not to laugh but ignored her instead.

"There's lots of different stuff in the cabinets; first day issue stamps, cigarette cards, medals, all sorts I've collected over the years. Tell you what, my son's wife Donna is coming for Christmas and my daughter Tess. You could each make something nice for them. They would really love that. We'll do it another day."

Chapter 12 Cora

Cora O'Brian stood in front of the mirror in her small house in Lambeth. She needed to look smart and professional but not too sassy. The more she looked, the more doubts entered her head. Finally, she decided she was fine. It was what she said that counted, not whether she was over dressed or not.

She was the lead child protection social worker for the London Borough of Greenwich and Lewisham and today they were interviewing for a new team leader overseeing social work for all vulnerable people. Sarah Jessop had done the job for over twenty years and was retiring in a few months' time. Cora felt she had a good chance; she certainly had the experience. She and Gary could certainly do with the extra money, they were really struggling at present. She heard the front door open downstairs.

"Bye Cora, good luck today." shouted Gary

"Bye Mum." shouted her two girls.

She ran downstairs and gave them all a hug and a kiss.

"Bye loves. Have a good day."

Going back upstairs she thought about how lucky she was to have Gary as her husband, he was a lovely man and a great dad. If she got this job she would be on top of the world. She'd do something really nice for the children. Perhaps take them to Alton Towers, everybody said it was really good and kids really loved it. Apparently all the girls' friends had been.

Cora was ready a good ten minutes before she needed to set off. As they often did, her thoughts turned to the past when she was growing up in Stepney. She'd had a great childhood, nice friends, and she did OK at school. Then when she was thirteen everything went wrong. A new girl joined the class called Carol. She was very cool; her dad was a musician in quite a well known band. Cora was never quite sure how it happened but her best friend, Joy, became Carol's friend and somehow all the other girls in her class turned against her. It was so upsetting, she would go home, go to bed early and cry herself to sleep.

She tried to keep it to herself, but her parents knew something was wrong and finally made her tell them. They were very understanding but couldn't really help. However, when they went to parents' evening and discovered her work had really deteriorated, they decided to act. They sent her to a private school in Brighton; she boarded Monday to Friday and her mum or dad brought her home for the weekend.

All went reasonably well for a year and one of the teachers, Mr Godfrey, was particularly kind and often took her to his office for a talk and to check she was OK. When they were alone, he insisted she called him Kevin.

One day Kevin called her to his office and told her that Dora's mum had contacted the school to say that the family dog had died. She wanted her to know before arriving home at the weekend. Cora was really upset and Kevin got her to sit on his lap and cuddled her. That was the start of him regularly abusing her. He was really clever and somehow made it seem that it was normal, and anyway, it was her that had started it.

It lasted two years and in the last few months the abuse turned to rape. She reported him and was labelled a liar and a troublemaker and told that, if she told her parents, she would be expelled and the school would sue her. However, the abuse stopped and Kevin left the school at the end of that term. Years later she managed to track him down.

When she met Gary and their relationship became serious, she told him that she had had a difficult time at school but that she would never tell him the details. This was partly because she didn't want anyone investigating what had happened to Kevin. It was typical of Gary; in all their married years he had never brought up the taboo subject; he must have wondered. She did feel that her childhood had made what was happening now all the better. Gary was wonderful and so were the girls, she was so lucky.

She checked all the doors and windows were locked as there had been a few break-ins in the street over the last year or so and set off. Leaving the house, she headed west towards the tube station, that would take her to New Cross and she would catch the bus to Lewisham. She could see a white van with an open sliding door a few yards ahead of her. Two men were looking into the van. As she walked past, Fenton turned towards her.

"Hello Cora, how're you doing?" he said smiling and then punched her hard in the face. She was stunned and a cloth was held against her mouth and nose. In seconds she was unconscious.

She was bundled into the van and Pamment followed her in. Fenton pulled the door shut, got in the driver's seat and started the engine. They drove about a mile to a small car park behind a cafe. They knew it didn't open for several hours and they had already checked there was no cctv in the area. There they took off the false plates, bagged them and threw them in a dumpster.

It had all gone to plan. Mr McBride would be very pleased.

Chapter 13 Christmas Eve

It was Christmas Eve and Daniel was playing Takoradi Bricks with Ben and his eldest son. Jake kept nudging Ben when he was trying to carefully remove a brick. Daniel wondered if Ben would get cross but he didn't seem to mind at all, come to think of it he couldn't really imagine Ben ever being cross. His daughter, Tess, and Lucy were sitting together reading a magazine. They seemed to be getting on really well. The rest of his family; his brother Mike, who lived on his own in Cornwall, youngest son Jason, and Donna, Jake's heavily pregnant wife, were sitting at the table discussing politics. It was great having his whole family together for Christmas and rare nowadays. He wondered if Ben and Lucy had something to do with them all coming.

Every three years they all went abroad for a week in the sun. Daniel organised it and paid for everything. It took him the three years to save up. They had a wonderful time swimming in the pool, eating great food, going to vineyards and taking trips to local places of interest. The last one had been a year and a half ago, near Avignon in Provence and they hadn't all been together since. In Daniel's opinion, the only thing that came above family was Harry. He had once told them that if one of them was walking down a road with Harry, and they saw an out of control lorry hurtling towards them, they should save Harry and sacrifice themselves. After all, he had three children but only one dog. They had laughed. The problem was, deep down, he feared he might actually mean it.

There was wine and soft drinks on the coffee table and also sandwiches and the remnants of a large chocolate cake. Ben had had three slices, that boy was insatiable and would probably be sick later.

"Your go, Dad, come on concentrate." said Jake.

Daniel carefully pulled out a brick and the whole tower collapsed.

"You are absolutely hopeless at this, Dad. Ben and I are embarrassed to have to play with you."

Ben giggled and Jake shook his hand.

"How dare you, just remember your place. Tess, Donna, Jason, you to Mike, come over here. Ben and Lucy, I am going to give you a family history lesson."

Ben and Lucy looked confused, the rest of those present groaned and did exaggerated yawns.

"Never mind about all that, Ben and Lucy, ignore them, they are ignoramuses, the lot of them, apart from Donna that is."

"What's an igiranus," asked Ben, looking confused.

Daniel explained, "It's a kind of cross between a hippopotamus and a rhinoceros, only pink. Now, gather round, you need to hear this.

"Our ancestors go back to the days when nomadic tribes roamed the countryside; hunting for buffalo, bison and hamsters, drinking from streams, digging for ....

"Get on with it, it'll be Easter before you've finished," shouted Jason.

Daniel turned to Jason and gave him a disdainful look.

"Be silent, you little apology for a subhuman being. Lucy, arrest that man immediately. Now where was I? Oh yes, our ancestors. They were clumsy and uneducated, a bit like Jake really. We all had sacred names in those days. I had several, being the big boss."

"More like Big head I would say." Muttered Tess to Lucy. Everyone laughed.

"Silence young whippersnapper," instructed Daniel loudly. "Me, big chief giant oak tree, him (Jake), my son, little stump.

"Me, big chief great lake, she (Tess) my daughter, muddy puddle."

Out of the corner of his eye, Daniel could see Ben and Lucy. Ben was smiling but looking quite confused. Lucy was loving it; he could see her laughing out loud. He had never seen that before.

"Me, Big Chief Mountain High, him (Jason) my son, little hillock.

"Little Pillock, more like," said Jake laughing.

A mock fight ensued between Jake and Jason with everyone else cheering them on. Daniel looked over at Ben and Lucy again. They were beaming with happiness, he almost cried. At that point, while everyone was watching Jake and Jason's antics, he quietly left the room. A minute later the doorbell rang and Daniel slipped back in. Tess went to answer the door.

Suddenly, she shouted, "Ben, Lucy, come and see, Father Christmas has left a bag of presents."

Ben and Lucy rushed out and when they returned they were pulling a huge black sack.

Daniel took control. "Now, let's get this organised. Jake, you take the presents out of the sack and call out who they're for, Tess, you show Lucy how to arrange them round the tree. Ben, you carry on running round in circles and then check everybody is doing their job properly. Harry, you have a lie down."

"Now let's see here," said Jake, "to little Pillock from Father Christmas. Oh, sorry I mis-read it, it actually says to Jason. To Donna from the elves. To Lucy from Rudolph. Well done, Lucy." Lucy beamed. "To, hey it's to me and it's the biggest so far. I think it might be a brand new Rolls Royce. One for Tess, another for Lucy."

While all this was going on Daniel was watching Ben. He was shaking with excitement and was genuinely pleased for everyone as their name was called out. But Daniel could also see his disappointment as he was being overlooked. He slipped out of the room again.

"Another small parcel for Donna, I reckon that must be a pram." He pulled out what was obviously a bottle. "One for Mike, no idea what that is, might be a book. One for Harry." They all looked over to Harry, who was fast asleep in front of the fire. "It's good to see you so excited, Harry. And that's the lot."

There was silence and everyone looked towards Ben who was doing his best to keep smiling.

Daniel re-entered and said. "That's not right, there must be another bag, go and look properly Tess, and, I mean, look properly this time."

Tess went out and returned with another bag of presents.

"Looks like Father Christmas must have forgotten to leave this one. He must have realised and come back with it," said Tess.

Daniel took out the present nearest the top.

"Well would you believe it; I can't quite make out the label."

"Get on with it Dad, the poor kid's nearly wetting himself," said an exasperated Tess.

"To Ben with love, from Father Christmas."

Ben was beside himself; he ran round in circles jumping up and down as he went. Everyone was laughing and hugging him. At that moment the doorbell rang. Daniel left to see who it was, he hoped it was carol singers, that would be the icing on the cake.

"What Christmas presents did you get last year, Lucy?" asked Tess.

Lucy looked down at the floor and muttered, "we didn't have any. Dad didn't like Christmas."

"We did have a mince pie," Ben said, "then Dad found out. He punched mummy; she fell on the floor."

Everyone in the room was staring at Ben and Lucy; there was a shocked silence.

It was Jackie at the door looking very serious.

"Come in, have a drink," said Daniel.

"No, no, I can't stop. Daniel I've got something to tell you, it's not good. The social worker who helped rescue the kids is missing. She left for an interview at work Monday morning and never arrived."

"Oh no, what was her name?" said Daniel.

"Cora O'Brian."

"It couldn't be coincidence, another reason or something else?"

"I'd love to think so but no, he's got her. The Met have no clues and certainly no evidence to tie it in with McBride. I would have left it until after Christmas but it will be on the news tonight."

"Jackie are we in danger?" asked Daniel.

"Look the only person who knows where they are is me, and the only person who knows I know is my friend in the met. But as a precaution, I'm going to text or ring you at nine in the morning and nine at night, every day. If you haven't heard from me by half past, get out of the house and get as far away as you can. I'm going to go. I'm sorry to bring you such horrible news on a day like today. Try to have a good Christmas. Bye."

When Daniel re-entered the living room it was surprisingly quiet.

Jason said, "Dad when we were little, you know, tiny tots, you always let us open one present on Christmas Eve. How about letting Ben and Lucy do the same?"

Daniel managed to put aside the huge weight he was feeling.

"OK, great idea young Jason, I'm glad I thought of it. Lucy, fetch the parcel with the green bow, that's for you, happy Christmas, Lucy."

Everyone cheered as Lucy carefully opened the present. A while back, Lucy had said that she really enjoyed art at school and Daniel had bought her a set of acrylic paints, pads of paper and some brushes. Lucy mumbled thanks and went to sit next to Tess; she had tears in her eyes and was obviously very emotional. Tess put her arm round her and hugged her.

"Ben, yours is the one at the front with the red ribbon," said Daniel.

It was big and Ben opened it slowly. it was a huge brown and white cuddly dog with a head very similar to Harry. Ben started sobbing and everyone looked at him and asked what was wrong.

Lucy answered affectionately, "He's never had a present before, he doesn't know what to do, silly wanker."

Daniel scowled at Lucy and wagged his finger. Lucy scowled and wagged her finger back at Daniel. He couldn't help himself but laugh. Lucy smirked. Ben stopped crying after a while and, hugging his dog, went and sat on the floor in a corner. Harry went over to sniff the new animal in the room and tried to wrest it off Ben. Daniel called him away. Jason joined Ben and put his arm round him. Everyone was much quieter now, there was an emotionally charged atmosphere in the room and tears in nearly everyone's eyes. Over the last five minutes the realisation had hit all of them as to what kind of lives these children had been living.

Daniel left the room and walked into the kitchen. He leant on the sink and looked out of the window. Finally, he got his mobile out and took his address book from the draw. He looked up a number and made a call.

"Hello, could I speak to Mickey Rance please ..... it's personal. Ah, Hello Mr Rance ..... Oh, OK, Mickey, I don't know if you remember me, I was your teacher once; Daniel Pitt ..... yeah it's nice to talk to you too ...... yes we did. Mr Rance ..... sorry, Mickey, is it OK to talk on this phone, what I have to ask you is quite delicate, maybe not for others to hear ..... OK, great. Please don't be offended but a friend told me you know a few local rogues still ..... yes that's right. Look, when you left school, you said to me that I had been the only teacher who had tried to keep you out of trouble, you know, put in a good word for you, believed in you. At the time you said that if I ever needed a favour, I was to ask ..... Thank you, that's nice of you to say so. Mickey I know from the papers you've done really well for yourself but back in the day you had some, let's be honest, some pretty scary friends ..... yes he was the scariest. I wondered if you still knew any of them. ...... Yes .... Yes. The thing is, well, I want to buy a gun."

He listened for a bit longer, thanked Mickey and then put the phone down.

He leant on the sink and stared into the garden. Lucy came in and Daniel turned. She looked at him for a few seconds, her eyes brimming with tears, then, ran up and put her arms out to him. Daniel dropped to his knees and took her in his arms and hugged her as hard as he could without hurting her. Apart from one handshake this was the first time there had been any physical contact between them. All her emotions surfaced and she sobbed into his chest. Jake and Ben appeared at the door. Jake left and Ben ran to Daniel and hugged him as well. As the children clung on to Daniel with all their strength, they let the fears and monsters that continually plagued them and gnawed at their souls, slowly disappear with the tears falling from their eyes. They bathed in the warm feeling of being safe, of being loved and of being happy. All Daniel could think to say was,

"There there, It's OK, there there."

Chapter 14 No Mercy

Cora lay huddled on the floor. When she had come round, she'd found that she was naked apart from a thin blanket over her. It was cold and she shivered every so often. She thought she was probably in a cellar, there was no natural light and both the floor and walls were stone. She was handcuffed to a metal ring screwed to the wall. She had no idea how long she had been there or what time of day it was. After what seemed hours, she heard a key rattle in the door and three men walked in. She pulled the blanket tightly about her.

McBride stared at her for a while and then spoke.

"Because of you, I will not be spending time with my adorable children this Christmas and, in case you are wondering, that is why you are here. Now you have a choice to make. You are going to die because of what you've done, that's a done deal. But what happens to your family, that's now up to you. If you cooperate and do exactly what you are told and make no attempt to escape or be difficult, then fine. That's the end of it. But, on the other hand, if you decide not to cooperate fully, then we will go after your husband Gary, your daughter Angela, your daughter Flora and your dad Stan and we will kill each and every one of them. And it will be drawn out and very, very painful. It's your choice. Give her some clothes."

Pamment stepped forward, unlocked the handcuff and threw some clothes and a brown wig on the floor next to her. She got dressed, trying to hide her nakedness as much as possible.

They took her out, up some stairs, through a door and onto a quiet street. Barry was sitting in a van waiting with the engine running. Pamment pushed her in the back and followed her in. Fenton got in the front. McBride watched until they were out of sight and then strolled back inside.

Barry drove for about an hour and finally reached the edge of a forest. Eventually he saw the dirt track he was looking for and drove down it for about a quarter of a mile. They didn't see anyone and pulled in among the trees. No one would be able to see the car unless they were very close to it. They pulled Cora out of the car and then walked down a small path into the forest.

"Come and give us a hand, Baz," shouted Pamment.

"Nah, I'll keep watch," replied Barry.

"What for, squirrels, you little prick?"

Eventually the path petered out but they walked a few hundred yards further through the trees until they came to a small clearing. A hole had been dug about three feet deep and two shovels had been left. There was also a large cardboard box about six feet long and two feet wide.

"Undress," said Don

Cora didn't move, she was absolutely terrified.

"Undress, now, remember what the boss said, so take everything off."

Cora was shaking with fear but did as she was told and undressed.

"Now lie in the box."

"No, please, please don't do this, hit me with a hammer, shoot me, strangle me but not this, please. Show some mercy, I've not hurt you. It was my job; I was just doing my job."

"Finished? Great speech, now GET IN!" Fenton shouted.

"Please."

"Get in, this is your last chance. Personally, I hope you refuse, I quite fancy having a bit of fun with your daughters, especially the younger one. How old is she, eight?, nine?"

Cora lay down in the box and Fenton and Pamment taped the lid on firmly. They picked up the box and dropped it into the hole. They could hear her sobbing and screaming. They picked up the shovels and filled the hole with earth. They could still hear her faintly so they waited. After a while the sound ceased. They gave it ten more minutes and then spread leaves and bits of greenery over the grave. Pamment moved away and looked back. There was no sign that anybody had been digging. They picked up the equipment and walked back to the car. On the way, they left a couple of cigarette buts, they had picked up from the gutter and in a service station, and also placed a single glove in bushes near the path. They hoped that one of them would have someone's DNA on it.

Pamment was furious, and when he got back, he pulled Barry out of the car and pushed him against a tree.

"What's the matter with you, Payne. Every time we have a job you wimp out and make an excuse. You do it one more time and I'll tell the boss."

Barry pushed him away.

"I'm the driver, I'm not paid to do the dirty work. You don't like it you're welcome to take it up with Mr McBride."

Pamment wanted to beat the shit out of him but Fenton put his hand on his shoulder and shook his head. They both knew that the boss would not be happy at all if they started fighting among themselves and, that was something to avoid.

They put all their gear in the boot and drove back down the lane. A quarter of an hour later they pulled into Oxted Quarry. It was evening and it was completely deserted, apart for a Ford Escort parked by the entrance. A man was sitting in the driver's seat. Fenton went over to it and the man got out and fetched three bags of clothes and shoes from the boot and gave them to him. Returning to their car, they then drove further in, got out and changed into the new clothes, placing the old stuff in the boot and leaving it open. Fenton doused the car with petrol, inside and out, and set fire to it. They waited to make sure no evidence could possibly have survived and then walked back to the Escort, got in, and three quarters of an hour later, the four of them were sitting in a drinking club in Deptford, where everyone present would swear they had been all evening.

Chapter 15 Memories

Jackie had a day off. She knew Ben and Lucy were at school so she rang Daniel to see if he fancied meeting up for lunch. They met at the 'Pride of the West', a Café in Puriton, round about halfway between Shipham and Taunton. Neither of them felt like lunch straight away; Jackie said she was watching her weight, so they just had coffee.

"Tell me about another funny tale from your days in teaching," said Jackie, leaning back on the comfortable chair. "Did you actually get any educating done between the jolly japes?"

"Very funny. Well, there was one really weird thing that happened.

"You could tell if you were losing the kids in a lesson; it usually happened because it was a boring topic or maybe too hard or easy for them, or perhaps, I wasn't presenting it very well. If that happened, I would stop ten minutes from the end and do something entertaining; quirky even, so they didn't leave with negative thoughts. Anyway, I had this small watering can and I used to half fill it with water and tell the pupils it was a brain cell recorder. So, I'd go up to a kid, put it against their ear and pretend to read a dial inside and tell him his score. Then as I was lifting the can away, I'd tip it slightly and pour water over them. The victims and those watching loved it. There was great hilarity."

"You are a very strange person!" Commented Jackie, dryly.

"Thank you, nice of you to say so. Anyway, I did it to a girl called Beatrice. She was a strange girl, a bit of a slob really. She never contributed anything in a lesson and seem to lounge about a lot. I had no relationship with her, as a teacher, at all.

Anyway, after I'd done it to her she looked up at me and said, 'I'm allergic to waer.' Everyone went quiet and I asked her what she meant. Too be honest I thought I'd mis-heard. 'waer, I'm allergic to waer.'

She stared at me without blinking and, before my eyes, the area that had got wet; her ear neck and arm, started turning pink, and then red. 'Follow me.' I said to her in an absolute panic and pulled her out of her chair and hustled her out of the room and down to the admin office. As I left, I shouted to the class that if anyone moved I would cut their legs off. I handed her over to our finance officer, Pauline Ham, who doubled as giver of first aid and rushed back to my class.

Beatrice was away for two weeks. I rang her mum to apologise and she said, in a dead pan voice just like Beatrice, 'Oh don't worry love, she's always been a bit of a plonker.'

My question is this: how on earth can you be allergic to water?"

"It is rather mind blowing, I must admit," said Jackie, laughing, "anymore?"

"I tell you what," said Daniel, "I never seem to stop entertaining you with stories from my fascinating past. Your turn for once."

Jackie thought for a moment.

"OK, when I was fairly new to the force, before I knew you, I was lucky enough to be seconded back to Cheddar as part of a team investigating a girl who had gone missing after she left school. They wanted my local knowledge. It wasn't long before we suspected that the girl had actually been abducted and possibly murdered."

"I remember that." said Daniel, "It happened just before I moved into the area. The killer's name was Jim Wilkins, I think."

"John, John Wilkins. A maths teacher like you, and Shelley Watkins was his victim. Actually, Shelley and her family lived in Shipham for a while but then moved to Cheddar. I'd attended the Kings of Wessex school a few years earlier; that's where it happened.

"It was at a point in the investigation where we weren't really getting anywhere. Anyway, overnight we got an anonymous call. A woman rang in and said her daughter had told her she'd seen Shelley kissing a girl from Shipham, name of Teresa Williams. It was a lunchtime and they were in one of the classrooms on their own. Apparently she walked in and they stopped and shouted at her to get out. A few seconds later, they came out and went their separate ways. Personally, I couldn't really see how it was relevant to the investigation but nothing could be ignored. So, I was sent to Shipham with a sergeant called Brady. He was a creepy bastard; thought he was God's gift to women. He liked to tell the women constables stuff with sexual innuendos and whenever he spoke to you, he looked at your tits, rather than your face. To be fair it wasn't just women he treated with no respect, we all heard his thoughts on blacks, gays, beggars and anyone who had the audacity to disagree with his views."

"Ya, I know the sort; there were a few of those in the schools I taught at."

"So, Brady was given the job and he told me I was to go with him. He said the boss wanted a woman to talk to the girl; two girlies together sort of thing. I didn't want to go but I didn't really have a lot of choice, he was a sergeant after all. I still remember his exact words: 'Wentworth, get yer knickers on and come with me. We've got to go lesbo hunting.' He threw me the car keys and told me I was driving.

"On the way he asked me what I thought about lesbianism and that sort of thing. I said to him not to take offence but I didn't really want to talk about my feelings about it with him. He said, 'Well, that tells a story.' and laughed. I was so cross, I told him it didn't tell him a damn thing, apart from the fact that I didn't want to talk about it.

"Anyway, we interviewed the girl and it turned out they weren't kissing; Teresa was squeezing Shelley's zits, you know, spots. Apparently she ran a little business at school doing it for some the girls. Weird eh? She charged twenty pence a zit. Right little entrepreneur.

"I really should have smelt a rat, because while we had been interviewing Teresa, she'd missed the school bus. So, I suggested we gave her a lift, we were going down to Cheddar anyway but Brady immediately intervened. He said he didn't think that would be appropriate and told Mrs Williams she would have to take her. At the time I couldn't understand why he'd done that.

"On the way back, Brady asked me to pull into the entrance to the old Shipham Quarry as he needed a piss, as he put it. He went behind a bush and, as he walked back, I could see his flies were unzipped. He got back in the car, leaned across me and removed the car key. I didn't know what he was doing. Then he said, 'All this talk of lesbians makes you feel quite horny, doesn't it?' and he put his hand on my thigh and slowly moved it up my tights. I was absolutely horrified and told him to stop. He told me not to be so daft, it wouldn't do any harm and I should remember, he could help me with my career. By now his hand was at the top of my thigh. Then he leaned over and tried to kiss me. I slapped him, pushed him away and managed to get the door open.

"Once I was out, I speed dialled the base number and Tariq Ayew, one of the admin workers, answered. I told him someone needed to come and pick me up, it was really urgent and to send someone straight away. He asked why, what had happened and I told him not to waste time asking questions, just to do it."

"God, what did you do then?" asked Daniel, genuinely shocked.

"Well, I saw Brady had got out of the car and was glaring at me, so I took out my baton and held it up for him to see, then I walked up the path towards the quarry. He shouted that I'd better not say anything and, that, even if I did, no one would believe me. He was red in the face with anger. His last words were. 'I won't forget this, you stupid bitch, you'll be sorry.' Then he got in the car and drove off."

"Wow, I feel angry just listening. Is that the end of the story?"

"Well actually, no. It has quite a violent end. Do you want to hear the rest?"

"Is the Pope a Catholic?"

"OK, well, go and order me another latte and a slice of that rather scrumptious chocolate cake they've got on display."

"Right, what happened to watching your weight?"

"It's been watched enough for one day."

Daniel walked over to the counter and ordered two coffees, Jackie's cake and a piece of cheese and ham quiche and asked the woman if it came with chips. She looked at him with disdain and, in a way that made me feel like he had just urinated on her counter, she said.

"Certainly not, it comes with salad,"

He sat down and looked at Jackie expectantly.

"OK," she said, "Round two. Brady was an absolute shit head but most of the people there were great. But it was our boss that made being on that team the most fantastic of experiences. Detective Chief Inspector Thomas was brilliant and demanded that everyone was both respectful and valued the work of others. Mind you, woe betide you if you got things wrong or were unprofessional.

"On my first day with the team, she called me and two other uniformed officers, who were also on secondment, into her office and asked us if we watched TV crime dramas. She asked if we had observed the way detectives treated uniformed officers, belittling them and calling them names, wooden tops for instance. 'Well,' she said, 'that sort of thing does not happen when I'm leading an investigation. We are a team and everyone has an important role to play and everyone has the right to be respected, no matter what their rank, colour or sexuality. But, most important of all, if you think you have something that could contribute to taking the case forward, you say it, however farfetched, no one will ridicule you. I want to hear your ideas.'

Anyway, when I got back to the base, there was no sign of Brady. I marched straight up to Thomas' door, knocked and walked in. I was shaking with anger but also really upset. I was struggling not to cry. Thomas was looking at a map with her inspector, a woman called Danby. I apologised for interrupting and asked for a few minutes of her time. I think she could see I was struggling to keep it together. Danby saw it too and without a word left the room and shut the door. Thomas signalled for me to sit down and then picked up her chair, carried it round and sat down next to me. She took my hand in hers and said, 'Tell me.'

"I tried not to be too emotional and told her exactly what had happened. Afterwards, Thomas patted me on the shoulder and opened her door, she called in a woman called Julie; she was one of the admin assistants, they are really vital to the management of an investigation.

"Thomas told Julie that I had had a very harrowing experience and that she wanted her to take me to the café in Cheddar for a coffee. Apparently, Julie was a councillor in her other life. She told me to tell her what happened and she would hopefully give me some good advice on how to handle it. She wanted some time to think about how to handle the situation and that we had to be back in an hour. Julie was great and when I got back I felt a lot calmer. Thomas was a lot more businesslike, not unkind just a bit more formal. She told me that a lot of the male officers on the force would not see what Brady did as particularly wrong, some of them even think that that's what the female officers are there for, that and to make them tea.

"She was not just talking about lower ranks, but all the way up to the top and that is why she would advise me not to report this to the top brass. She said it would do my career no good at all. I remember her saying, 'It's wrong, I know it's wrong, and, you know it's wrong but it's the way it is.' So, what she proposed was that she would speak to Brady and have him sign a statement as to what had happened. She would then give him a verbal caution and warn him about his future conduct. If there was any further incident a report would go straight to the chief constable and he would inevitably be sacked without a pension, because then it would be her, a chief inspector making the complaint. She asked me what I felt about that."

"So, what did you say?" asked Daniel.

"I told her I totally trusted her and was happy do whatever she thought was best.

"She told me she was not going to ask him to apologise, that would be an empty gesture, and then, hard as it may seem, we were all going to carry on as if nothing had happened and not talk about it to anyone. The exception was, if I needed help, I should go to Julia. She showed me the report she'd written of the incident and asked me if it was accurate or if she'd left anything out. I read it through and signed it. Finally, she said that I would not be teamed up with Brady for any reason, at any time in the future.

She then told me to move my chair to the back of the room, to sit down and not to interrupt, whatever happened. She went and got Brady and, when he walked in, he looked at me with such hatred, I actually felt quite scared.

"He sat down facing Thomas but she told him to stand until he was told otherwise and handed him the report and told him to read it. After a couple of lines, he started protesting his innocence but she told him to be quiet and to read it all the way through. He got really agitated, kept muttering to himself. Finally, he put it down and said, 'Guv, it's a pack of lies, she's always had it in for me, she's a pain in the arse.' Thomas interrupted him and said, 'Detective Sargent Brady. Stop it right now. We both know that it is not a pack of lies; that it is absolutely the truth, so stop the facade and sign the document. If you do, I'm going to give you a verbal warning and the document you have just signed will remain under lock and key. No one else will know of your indiscretion. However, I'm going to tell you straight, if, in the future, I hear even a whisper that you have acted inappropriately with a female member of staff or a member of the public, that document goes straight to the chief constable. Do you understand me. Now let me be clear, if you don't sign it, I will have you arrested now, in front of all your colleagues, and charge you with sexual assault. You will go to court and, win or lose, your career will be finished and everybody will know why.'

Brady thought for a moment, and then said that his rights were being ignored and he wanted to speak to a rep from the Police Federation before he even thought about signing.

'Fine,' she said, 'Constable Wentworth, please handcuff the prisoner. Liam Brady, I am arresting you on a charge of sexual assault. You do not have to say anything but ..... He interrupted her and said, 'alright, alright. I'll sign the fucking thing.' Thomas withheld the pen and just sat there staring at him. Finally, he caught on and apologised for swearing and then he signed it. I was sent out at that point and Danby was asked to come in.

I went to my desk and started reading through a witness statement. I have to admit, I was quite worried about what would happen when Brady came out and walked past me; he was bound to say something horrible; he might even attack me. I took out my baton and put it across my knees, hidden under the table. I made a decision that I was not going to be cowed or intimidated by that shithead. It wasn't me who'd assaulted him. About five minutes later there was a loud noise and a cry from Thomas' office. Everyone looked up. The next thing we knew, Thomas and Danby came out of the office helping

Brady who was doubled over and obviously in great pain. He had blood pouring from his face. Thomas called over a couple of officers and told them that Brady had had an accident; tripped and fell over and may have broken his nose. She told them to take him to casualty at Weston Hospital to get him patched up. She said they were to drop him off but not to wait for him, he could get a taxi back. As she walked past my desk back to her office, she stopped beside me and said quietly something that I didn't really understand at the time. She said, 'there, he's got me to hate now, hopefully he won't bother about you anymore,' and then walked on."

"Blimey, did you ever find out what happened?" asked Daniel.

"Oh yes. Danby told me quite a lot later when I'd become a detective constable. Apparently after I'd left, Thomas had stood in front of Brady and then, without any warning, she'd brought her knee up, catching him fully in the groin. Brady had been taken completely by surprise, as had Danby, and as he started to bend over double in agony, she brought her knee up again right into his face. Danby said she had clearly heard the crack as his nose broke. He collapsed to the floor moaning. Apparently Thomas stood over him and said, 'that was personal, from me to you, call it payment for saving your career."

"No way!" said Daniel, absolutely astounded by what he had just heard.

"Oh yes," said Jackie, "and, ever since that day Daniel, Detective Chief Inspector Thomas has been, and always will be, my all-time hero and the person I most aspire to be like."

Jackie stared into space for a while. "Well, I must go. You know, Thomas had me transferred to her team after that case. I became a detective. You see, in the end, we worked out who the killer was but we couldn't find him. Believe it or not I did some quite nifty detecting and found the bastard."

"How?"

"Another day. By the way, in case you didn't know, Thomas is now the first ever female Chief Constable of Somerset and Avon police constabulary."

Chapter 16 1850

It was six o'clock on a Sunday in mid-January and Daniel had woken up early. Harry wasn't really allowed to sleep on the bed at night but in the winter he did add a bit of warmth, so Daniel didn't make a fuss. The trouble was, during the night, he expanded his territory so Daniel was left with about six inches on the edge of the bed. Daniel pushed him over to his own side and, as usual, couldn't believe how heavy Harry could make himself when he felt like it. The dog let out a menacing growl.

He was just on the verge of going back to sleep when the door flew open and Ben and Lucy charged in. They jumped on the bed and Daniel quickly tried to bury himself under the covers. Harry obviously sensed who the likely winners of this battle would be and joined the kids' gang.

The children started chanting, "king of the bed, king of the bed……."

After a few minutes Daniel realised that he was on the verge of being pushed to the floor and couldn't win this particular battle, so he decided on a different tactic.

"Right, that's enough, Harry needs his morning walk. Enough, I said. What do you want for breakfast?"

"Fish, chips and Yorkshire puddings please," said Ben, laughing.

"You little rascal." Lucy said, and tousled his hair and gently slapped him.

"Ow, Daniel, punish her, she's beating me up. She's

a weirdo." He made a face at Lucy.

"Oh my God," exclaimed Lucy, "look at that, out of the window."

Ben looked and Lucy immediately pushed him on to his front, sat astride of him and tickled him. Ben was very ticklish and writhed and screamed for help. Daniel picked Lucy up and deposited her on the floor, next to Harry.

"Now, going back to my original question. What do you want for breakfast?"

"Cornflakes, please." said Ben.

"Fish, chips and Yorkshire puddings." said Lucy with a grin.

Daniel sighed, got back into bed, and pulled the covers over his head. Ben, Lucy and Harry immediately jumped on top of him.

They went to Charterhouse and parked in the small car park. It was still early and there were no other cars. Daniel took them on the forest path and, as they left the trees, there was a small lake to the right of the path. Harry climbed down the bank and into the water in order to have a drink. The children threw sticks to try and get him to fetch them. Harry wasn't interested and when he got out of the lake, he had a good shake, soaking Ben in the process.

"Is that why they call you squirt?" said Daniel. Nobody else laughed. "Come with me I want to show you something."

He took them to a long fenced off piece of land with what looked like four half chimneys in it. The chimneys, however, were along the ground rather than in the air. Ben picked up a piece of shiny black rock and showed it to Daniel.

"Why is it so shiny?"

"This is a piece of rock that has been placed in a very hot fire. There's tons of it around here. You see, this area has been mined for lead and silver for thousands of years, even before the Romans came; in the end there wasn't enough left to make it worthwhile, so they stopped. Look, I've brought along a piece of galena. Its lead in its natural form when it's been dug out of the ground. Feel how heavy it is." Both children held it. "Anyway, about two hundred years ago, some miners from Cornwall invented a new way of getting more lead from rocks that had already been worked. They built those chimneys on their sides that you can see there. They used bricks made at a quarry not far from here. At the entrances to each chimney, they built huge fires and put the rock, called slag, onto the fires. Then using big machines called bellows, they blew the smoke along the inside of the chimneys. The smoke had particles of lead in it and that stuck to the inside of the tunnels as a sort of slime. The rock you found Ben, is what is left after it had been burnt. Children from the workhouse were used to collect the lead."

"What's a workhouse?" asked Lucy.

"Well, this is the horrible bit. In those days some people were so poor that when they had children, they often couldn't afford to look after them and feed them, so they sent them to what was called the workhouse. They were terrible places. The children did not have a happy life and were not looked after very well and the food they were given was truly disgusting, to be honest, nobody really cared about them at all."

"So how were they used to collect the lead?" asked Lucy.

Daniel thought for a send or two.

"I tell you what, I wrote a short story about it once from the point of view of one of the children. I'll read it to you when we get home."

"I'd rather hear it now; Meany." Said Lucy

"Meany! How dare you. You should be grateful Harry didn't hear you say that, he would have ripped your throat out. Talking of Harry, where is the little devil?"

"He's a big devil to me," said Ben.

"That's really sad about those poor children in the workhouse," said Lucy. "Anyway Ben, even a mouse would look big to you – squirt."

She ran off with Ben chasing her.

"I'm going to give her a bunch of sixes, you wait. Come back."

That evening, when they were in bed, Daniel read his story.

"It's called eighteen sixty.

"I think I am eight years old and that my mother's last name was Jenkins. She died as I was being born. They never gave me a first name so I am just Jenkins. I have never known what it is to be loved, or any other life than this, so I don't really know if there is a better world out there. Just hints sometimes; laughter, singing or bells ringing in the distance.

There are twenty-six of us in all, but this often changes. Six days a week we are taken from the workhouse in Axbridge where I live and marched five miles to a lonely place where there are empty stone buildings, some in ruins. The rocks here are black and shiny. It is called Charterhouse and, when we arrive, we are each given a wooden spatula and a bucket. We are then sent into long tunnels, each one the shape of a chimney that has been built along the ground instead of in the air. We have to work on our hands and knees or lying on our backs. That is where I am now.

It is dark in here; I would be frightened if it weren't for the others close by. I can smell their sweat and the filth on their clothes and skin. I can see nothing, well perhaps a faint orange glow if I look back, but I prefer to keep my eyes closed, then grit or worse won't get in them and make them sore. I can hear the fire though, a dull drone and then the whoosh of the bellows which makes it roar and crackle. Smoke billows through, thick and acrid. It gets in our throats if we breathe in and each of us has to stop and cover our mouth and nose until it falls away.

I can feel the heat from the fire. On cold days, that is good, it warms my body. But today the sun is shining and my skin feels hot and raw. My body itches all over. I want to stop and scratch but if I don't get my quota done, I will be beaten with sticks.

The smoke leaves a thin layer of slime on the brickwork and it feels good, as I push the spatula along and the goo slurps into my bucket. My friend Jo is in front of me, she cannot smell the slime but I can. It smells of soot but also a sweet metallic tang, a bit like the pipes in our dormitory but not quite the same.

Hours go by and at midday we are allowed out and taken to a dirty pond nearby. We are given half a slice of mouldy bread and we drink from the pond. I love this, I go right in and put my head under the cold water, my itches ease and I drink my fill. It is bliss. If they aren't looking, I splash Jo and she returns the favour. After a few minutes they chase us back up the hill, back to work.

I do not know what it is I collect in my bucket, nor why it is of use, although I did hear one of the guards talk of lead, but I think it is some kind of poison as the pain in my gut is getting worse and worse. I can hardly eat the boiled gristle and hard bread they give us morning and night. Worst of all is the coughing. I cough all the time and sometimes it is so bad I am sick and cannot breathe. Sometimes, it stops me sleeping. I am in terrible pain now and feel so weak as I slide my spatula along the walls; I know the walk back will be dreadful.

Perhaps I will die soon and then I will meet my mother. She will hug and kiss me and take away my pain. Perhaps she will let me bring Jo. I can feel the wetness of tears on my cheeks. I don't know what to do."

The children lay in silence for a while.

"That's such a sad story," said Lucy.

"Yes, so, you should be grateful you have Harry and I to look after you," said Daniel. "Anyway, we'd better finish with something a bit more upbeat, did I ever tell you about when Colin Crocodile and Dino Dinosaur had a tug of war to see who the strongest animal in the forest was?"

Ben and Lucy shook their heads.

"Good. Well, here we go then."

Chapter 17 Investigation

Jackie was sitting in her office, feeling very frustrated. Sometime earlier, Daniel had given her a copy of his latest book, 'The Clue'. It was a crime drama based in a fictional school in Wells, called The Cathedral Academy. A fourteen year old girl had gone missing following a school band practice. It was the first draft and Daniel had asked her, if she had time, to read it through and let him know what her thoughts were, particularly, of whether the technical side of the investigation was realistic.

Jackie worked a minimum of ten hours every day and sometimes as much as fourteen hours, often six days a week. The idea of reading a book, making notes and then giving someone a heads up as to what was wrong with it, made her feel quite ill; she just didn't have time. But on the other hand, she knew how important it was to Daniel and he was a really kind, lovely man who would always help her if it was needed. Taking on Ben and Lucy had been a massive thing to do. He loved his writing and she knew he really wanted the book to be as true to life as possible.

To be fair to Daniel, he was a good writer. She had read his previous book while on leave and had really enjoyed it. It was about him spending two years in a remote village in Papua New Guinea when he was eighteen. He'd had the most extraordinary adventures.

What she'd read so far of his latest one was quite good but she knew he was expecting her to go into the technicalities of the investigation and that would take a lot of time. She had read the first couple of chapters and, already, she realised he had no idea how an investigation worked.

He had his lead character, a chief inspector out interviewing people and doing grunt work. A lot of that type of work would be done by uniformed constables, not even detectives. When she was leading an investigation she rarely got out of her office except when an important lead emerged that she needed to see firsthand. Even interviewing suspects or key witnesses was done by specially trained officers who would do it much better than she would. In most crime investigations, there would be hundreds of interviews and statements taken. Each one had to be written out meticulously. When there was a major crime, civilians were brought in to help with that.

All that information ended up on the lead investigator's desk, usually an inspector or chief inspector. Their job was to read and digest all of it, to have a full picture of everything that had been unearthed and acting on this to prioritise the immediate work of the team and the direction the investigation would take. They needed to be on top of everything. It could be the tiniest detail that broke a case wide open and it was often her job to find it.

The problem was, she owed Daniel big time. He had helped move a massive case forward that she had been working on for some time and she had ended up getting all the credit.

She had been given a special assignment. Over the past four years there had been five suspicious deaths in the

Avon and Somerset area. All the victims had been very good looking women, aged between twenty five and forty five. For one of the women, the pathologist was one hundred percent certain that she had been murdered and a full investigation had taken place. The other four, however, were less certain, they could easily have been accidental deaths or even suicides in two of the cases. Her boss had given Jackie the task of seeing if there was some kind of link between the women and, so far, she had failed to find any connection at all.

They had all led very different lives. Lettie Tresize was a theatre director who had been working at the Western Playhouse. Carmel Heriot was an author, who had just completed her fourth novel to critical acclaim. Amy Blakehouse, was a specialist cake maker, working from her own small café in the village of Stonyfield. Elin Abbot oversaw procurement at county hall in Taunton and Toni Racklin worked in the RSPCA charity shop In Winscombe. They just didn't seem to have anything in common.

She had talked over the case with Daniel; she wasn't supposed to but he was a good listener and would often come up with something useful. He had been sure the names were familiar but couldn't think why.

Then, two days later, he had rung her, sounding very excited, he'd told her he had cracked the case. All those five women had been interviewed on the BBC's local station View West. It was a sort of events and news program, local to Bristol, Gloucestershire, Somerset, Dorset and Avon. He remembered seeing the women clearly. An old pupil of Daniel's, James McGinty, who he had kept in touch with, was a freelance camera man and he and his partner had the contract to film the studio parts of View West. Because of James' involvement, Daniel never missed it. Once he realised where he'd seen the women he contacted James and got the details. All the interviews had taken place within the last four years and in each case the interviewer was the same person, the gorgeous Dawn Mockford, everyone's pinup girl.

Jackie asked Daniel if he wouldn't mind contacting James again and checking if he could remember anything unusual or untoward happening; arguments, accusations; anything? The answer was nothing, it was a friendly, non-controversial show and there were rarely any incidents and none that he could remember concerning those women.

Daniel suggested that she should concentrate on Dawn Mockford; find out if she had been stalked in the last two or three years or had had any other similar problems. However, when Jackie spoke to her on the phone, she said she wasn't aware of ever being stalked or followed. She said she was very careful, she never walked alone after dark and the BBC always provided her with a car and driver to take her to and from work.

That seemed to be the end of the road for that line of enquiry. And yet, she felt in her gut that there was something there. Apart from anything else, Daniel's intuition was rarely wrong. She decided to take a chance. The following day she presented a plan to her boss, Chief Inspector Gerald Manley.

Stakeouts are expensive but he gave the go ahead for a limited operation for a period of two weeks. And so, for the next fortnight, Dawn Mockford's movements were monitored. After just a few days they had a breakthrough. A man in a car, parked about fifty metres from her driveway, was observed on several occasions. When she came out in the morning he produced binoculars and appeared to be watching her walk down to the car that was waiting to drive her to work. He then drove off. He did not try to follow her. Over the next week he did the same thing once in the morning and once in the evening when she arrived home from work. His name was Bradley Johnston and he lived in a flat in Barton Hill high rise, in Saint Philips in Bristol. Jackie was sure this was the killer and it must be to do with all the women being beautiful but she had absolutely no evidence.

After much thought, she went back to Gerald Manly with plan B. The possibility of his team arresting a five times killer was enough for him. He knew that this was the stuff that promotions were made from.

Two weeks later, on View West, Jean Mockford interviewed Jenny Brown, who was an avid watcher of the program. She had raised twenty five thousand pounds for charity by walking around the perimeter of the View West catchment area. Jenny was stunningly beautiful and with her vibrant personality, really stole the show. During the interview Jenny had revealed that she worked for ASDA and lived in Bedminster on the outskirts of Bristol.

Jenny Brown was actually a uniformed constable who loved a scrap. She was fearless and volunteered for everything, the more dangerous the better. She had turned down the chance of promotion because she wanted to be at the front line; In the city centre on a Saturday night, dishing out some agro, as she put it. She had jumped at the chance to work Jackie's sting.

For two weeks Jenny worked as a shelf filler at ASDA, and afterwards walked home in the winter's gloom. On the fifteenth night Jackie was beginning to think she must have got it wrong. Jenny was nearly home when a car pulled up next to her. The driver had his window down and was pointing a gun at her face. In his other hand he held a cloth that had a chemical smell emanating from it. Jenny knew that if he got that cloth over her mouth and nose she would be helpless and rendered unconscious in seconds. At that moment sirens could be heard from two directions. As he turned to look, Jenny grabbed the gun with one hand and punched him in the face with the other.

Two police cars shot into the road and skidded to a halt, preventing Johnston's car from moving. Within a few seconds, Jackie and a host of officers, some armed, had surrounded the scene. They were not needed, however. Jenny was standing looking down at her assailant who was groaning with his hands handcuffed behind his back. He looked very sorry for himself and had blood trickling from is nose and mouth.

"Give me five minutes with him guv, I'll get a full confession."

Jackie laughed, "Nice idea and I'm tempted, but no, we really need him alive, or at least in a fit state to talk."

Jenny grinned, she liked Jackie; she wasn't stuck up like a lot of the brass and she didn't stare at her breasts either.

When he was interviewed, it turned out Jackie had been spot on. Johnston had been watching Jean for years and that was enough for him; he didn't feel the need to get close up. But when the future victims were being interviewed by her, he became angry, he felt they were demeaning her with their beauty. He couldn't allow that, and so he killed them. The one surprising thing was that Johnston was well educated. He had gained a master's degree in mechanics from Imperial College and, at one time, had a job with Rolls Royce in Bristol; now though, he was unemployed and totally obsessed.

There was easily enough evidence to charge Johnston with two counts of murder and one of attempted abduction. In the end he pleaded guilty to all five murders and received a whole life prison sentence. Jenny Brown and Jackie were commended and Gerald Manley got his promotion.

The next time Jackie met Daniel she apologised that she couldn't give him the credit he deserved. Without his input they might never have solved the case. Typically, he laughed and said that he didn't need or want any credit and congratulated her. He said he was sure that she would have got him in the end anyway.

'I'll skip a night's sleep,' she thought, 'I'll help him with his bloody book.'

Chapter 18 The Warning

On the ground floor of Justin McBride's headquarters in New Cross there was a large storage space. It was usually fairly empty but today there were seven men standing and waiting nervously for their boss. Among them were Barry Payne, George Pamment and Don Fenton. When McBride walked in he was carrying a knife and an apple.

He sat down behind an old wooden table and leisurely peeled the apple, cut pieces off and ate them. When he had finished he tossed the apple core into a wastepaper basket and, with a great deal of venom, stuck the knife into the desk. He looked at each of the men in front of him in turn, burning into them with his dark eyes, that exuded hatred and contempt.

"Jarvis, why are you all here?" he said.

"I, I don't know boss."

"Is that right Jarvis, you don't know?"

"No boss, sorry boss."

"Oh well, I'm glad you're sorry, that's just what I want to hear, that you're fucking sorry."

Jarvis decided the best thing to do was to stay silent.

"Pamment, tell Jarvis why he's here, he might worry otherwise and I wouldn't want to see him worried."

"Cos we haven't found your kids boss."

"Gold star for you, Pamment. That's right. My dear children, who should be at home with me, are out there somewhere and I don't know where. Even Christmas day, it was just me sitting at home in front of the Christmas tree and singing carols all on my lonesome. Well at least Pamment and Fenton have done something, they found the social worker who took them away. Funnily enough she didn't manage to spend Christmas with her kids either. She was missing, sort of went underground.

"But what I don't understand is this. Your job was to find the police officers who took them from the house, the person who took them to wherever they are being hidden and, finally, the person who's got them now. In fact, anyone involved in their abduction. None of those things have happened. Now get out of my sight and do your fucking jobs."

They left. McBride sat, steaming with frustration. 'Perhaps I'll make an example of one of them soon,' he thought to himself.

Chapter 19 Incest training

Daniel noticed that the kids always seemed to come home from school in good humour. He didn't remember his own kids doing that, not every day anyway. Ben and Lucy both seemed to love school. There was the usual pandemonium as Harry greeted them, acting as if it was the best thing that had ever happened to him. The children loved it and didn't mind being knocked over, trod on and having their faces licked all over. Eventually, Harry would flop down on his bed, exhausted. One Thursday, Ben had some unusual and quite worrying news for Daniel.

"We have the day off tomorrow; our teachers have an incest training day."

Daniel, who was drinking a cup of coffee, spluttered and soaked the front of his shirt. He looked at Lucy but she hadn't reacted at all. However, both were looking at Daniel, with his coffee soaked clothes, as if he was crazy.

"I think you mean INSET training day. Actually, I already knew that, being a man of much higher than average insight and intelligence and, as it's a Friday tomorrow, and you don't have to get up for school the next day, I thought we'd go to the cinema tomorrow evening. Willy Wonka and the Chocolate Factory is on, a bit young for you but I thought I might like it."

"I'd really like that," said Lucy.

"Me to," chimed in Ben, "can Harry come?"

"No, he doesn't like films. He's more a theatre loving pooch; William Shakespeare and Samuel Becket, that sort of thing."

"Who is Samuel Bucket?" asked Ben.

"Samuel Becket numbskull, he wrote Waiting for Godot."

Daniel was astonished, "Wow Lucy, I know you're a clever girl but how on earth did you know that?"

"One of dad's men, Barry; I think he was dad's driver. He used to go to the theatre a lot with his mum and he often told me about the plays he'd seen or read. Would you take me to see a play, Daniel?"

"I definitely will Lucy."

"I liked Barry," said Ben, "apart from mum, he was the only person who was kind to us. He used to give us chocolate and sweets sometimes."

"We always had to promise not to tell dad though, he would probably have killed him if he'd found out," said Lucy.

Not for the first time, Daniel got a sinking feeling. These kids had had such awful treatment at the hands of their father and it was not inconceivable, that sometime in the future, they would be back in his hands.

The following morning it was cold but sunny. The three humans and one nearly human were outside and three of them were wrapped up warm and sitting on garden chairs. Lucy was giving Harry an ear tickle and every time she stopped, he nudged her until she carried on. It made both her and Ben giggle.

"Don't laugh at him, he gets very angry and could easily rip out your throat and kill you. Probably eat you as well."

They all looked at Harry who was looking very dangerous with a sort of grinning expression and his tongue hanging out.

Lucy returned to her ear tickling duties and Daniel continued his intellectual discussion with Ben as to the merits of tomato ketchup over mayonnaise, on chips.

Lucy looked up, "I think I can hear the phone ringing Daniel."

"I'll go," said Ben.

"No. I'll go," said Daniel. He was reluctant to allow Ben or Lucy to answer the phone.

He picked up and said, "Hello, Daniel Pitt here ..... oh yes, hi ..... you have, when? ..... Yes, that's great, we can make that, what do you need us to bring? ..... OK, we'll be there in about half an hour, bye."

He walked to the patio door.

"Hey kids," he called out, "You are the lucky ones. Cinema this evening and another treat this morning. You are going horse riding. That was Georgina, at the stables in Broadway, they've had a cancellation and we can have the slot for half the normal price."

"Will you buy us sweets and ice creams with the other half?" asked Lucy.

Daniel was always really impressed with her quick thinking and sense of humour, which was not unlike his own.

"In your dreams, kiddo." was his retort.

As usual, Lucy accepted his decision in a thoroughly adult manner and stuck her tongue out at him.

Georgina was there to greet them when they arrived. She took the children into the saddle room and gave them some equipment to try on. Once she was satisfied they were properly kitted out, she called to the stable girl, Imani, to bring out the first horse.

"I've always wanted to ride a horse. Thanks, Daniel," said Lucy.

Ben looked at the horse and said nervously, "He's very big, isn't he."

"Don't worry sweetheart," said Georgina, "that's not yours. Here's your pony."

Ben thought even this one looked big but he didn't say anything. He didn't want Lucy laughing at him.

"Now Ben," said Daniel, "you will ride your pony to the far end of the field and then the pony will ride you on the way back. That's only fair."

"Ignore him," said Georgina, "the horse doesn't ride you. This is Cheeky, Ben, and Lucy, yours is called Sonya."

Daniel chimed in. "Now Lucy, Sonya ...."

"Be quiet Daniel, the children are nervous enough without you making things worse," said Georgina, in a very stern voice.

Lucy laughed and gave Georgina a high five. It was fun seeing Daniel being told off. Daniel pretended to sulk.

"Ok children, don't be worried, for your first lesson both horses will be on a rope, you'll just do the basics; get to know your horse and let them get to know you. The important thing is, not to be scared and to enjoy yourselves. OK, I'll show you how to mount."

Georgina helped them mount and then led them through the gate to the field beyond. All the time she was telling them about the reins and how to get your horse to stop or turn. She encouraged them to talk to their horses and pat them as often as they could.

She had the ability to make it all sound really simple, which helped take away the children's nerves.

It wasn't long before she let the rope out and had them trotting, stopping and turning. Daniel, having been reprimanded once, kept his distance but took lots of photographs.

Finally, an hour later they rode back to the stable yard and dismounted.

"Did you enjoy that?" asked Georgina.

"It was great," said Ben.

"I really enjoyed it," said Lucy, "but I wish we could have galloped."

"There's an old saying: You can't run until you can walk. You wait, you'll be galloping in no time."

"Thanks, Georgina and Imani, I'll ring you to book some more sessions. Bye."

"Bye, Georgina, Imani," shouted the kids.

"Bye Sonya and Cheeky," shouted Ben.

Sonya and Cheeky ignored him, they were too busy munching the carrot Georgina had given them.

That evening they arrived for Willy Wonka and the Chocolate Factory with plenty of time to spare. Daniel paid for the tickets and bought a tub of popcorn for each of them. Daniel did not think he had ever seen the children so excited.

The cinema was about a third full and Daniel chose some seats to the side, not too near anyone else. The kids chose to sit either side of him, and Lucy put her arm through his and squeezed. At that moment, a warm but painful feeling surged through Daniel. The realization hit him that he'd fallen in love with these children and he would do anything to protect them. He didn't want them to go anywhere else. He shook his head, 'I mustn't think like this, it will only lead to pain,' he told himself.

"So, what films have you seen before?" he asked.

Ben was so busy looking round in awe at his surroundings, he didn't answer. Or, maybe, it was because his mouth was full of popcorn.

"We've never been to a cinema," said Lucy quietly, "we weren't allowed."

It was a good job they had sat apart. The children totally immersed themselves in the film, jumping up and down, laughing out loud and cheering Charlie on. They had an absolutely wonderful time. Daniel didn't have a TV but he decided that a visit to the cinema once a month would be a really good thing to do.

As they left, Ben was trying hard to remember the lyrics to one of the songs and sing it.

"Oompo oompa dubity doo
Oomp oompa dubity dap."

"Be quiet dumbo or I'll butt your balls off," said Lucy.

"And I'll cut you tits off, back," replied Ben making a face at her.

They were in a crowd and a number of people were turning round to look at them, all looking rather shocked.

"Hey, you two," said Daniel, "balls and tits are not things to be discussed while other people are about, they'll think you're yobos from London."

"Well, I suppose we are really," said Lucy laughing.

"Yes, well, we don't want the police to arrest you for yobbish behaviour; I believe the sentence for that is five thousand years in prison and no pocket money for a week."

Ben looked at Lucy a little confused. "We don't get any pocket money, do we?"

"Good point Ben and well argued," said Daniel, making Ben look even more confused. "I thought that was a really good film. I think my favourite bit was when the lift exploded into the sky. What about you, Ben?"

Ben thought for a moment. "I liked it when the big boy fell in the chocolate and got stuck in the tube."

"Yes that was funny. What about you, super slob, sorry, I mean Lucy?"

"I liked the Oompa Loompas best, they reminded me of Ben."

"If I'm an Oompa Loompa then you're a, a" he thought for a second, "a Dumpa Poopa." He stuck his tongue out at Lucy.

"Enough, heavens above, walking with you two is like walking with a pack of hyenas."

"Where are we going?" asked Lucy, who had just realised they had walked past the car.

"Ah well, I feel a bit lazy and I can't be bothered to cook this evening for a pair of wombats like you, so I thought we'd have a nice Chinese. The place over there does a cheap and decent buffet."

"What's a buffet?" asked Ben.

"It's where you help yourself, stupid," said Lucy.

"Don't call Ben stupid Lucy, it's not nice. Call him nincompoop, it's much more refined."

"I'm not stupid, you're both stupid and I'm not a numbercoop."

"The good news is, it's an 'eat as much as you want' restaurant." said Daniel, ignoring Ben, "you can go back for more, as many times as you like."

"Wow, I'm going back for more at least fifty times, I'm starving," said Ben.

"What about Harry?" said Lucy, "isn't it a long time to leave him?"

"It is," said Daniel, "but I asked Claire, who lives next door, if she would pop in and sit with Harry for a couple of hours. She has a key and I sometimes babysit for her when she needs me to."

They walked on and Lucy took Daniel's hand.

Twenty minutes later, they were sitting in the restaurant next to the window. Daniel and Lucy had put a variety of small portions of Chinese food on their plates. Ben had mainly chips and a few noodles.

Lucy looked over at Ben. "What's the point of going to a Chinese restaurant and then just eating chips?"

"I like chips, anyway I had some of those wormy things; snoodles."

"Noodles, dumbo," Lucy said, laughing.

They all started giggling at the word snoodles.

"Well," said Daniel, "I'm still hungry, so I'm going to get some more snoodles and maybe a few fried poodles as well."

Daniel went over to the food counters and started filling his plate with more food. Ben had obviously eaten enough chips and was watching the crowds out of the window. Suddenly, he saw someone he recognised.

"Look Lucy. There's Uncle Barry, and there's Don."

"Don't be stupid. Oh no! Ben, get your head down, NOW."

She ran up to Daniel. "Two of dad's men are out there, what do we do?"

For a second Daniel couldn't take it in, "Lucy are you absolutely sure?"

"Yes it's them, I saw them, Ben saw them as well."

"Ben, come over here," said Daniel, "and don't look towards the window. Right, listen carefully, they obviously know we're here somewhere but don't know exactly where. Now, do exactly what I tell you. Lucy, take Ben into the toilets, go into a stall and wait. If anybody comes for you apart from me, you scream for help, and you keep screaming, biting, kicking, do anything you can. Do not let them take you if you can help it. Keep fighting, help will come. It's going to be OK Ben, they're not going to find us, I promise. Before you go Lucy, can you see them now?"

Lucy looked, "Yes, only one of them, he's over there with a grey baseball cap and black jacket, that's Barry."

"Yes, I see him. OK. I'll be back soon. Go, GO."

Daniel took out his phone and called Jackie, making sure he could see Barry all the time.

"Jackie, we've got some trouble, I'm in a Chinese restaurant near the cinema at Hengrove, the children have just seen two of McBride's men ..... Definitely two and possibly more, they're outside looking for the kids ..... They're both in the toilets in the restaurant we were eating in .... Yes, I'm sure, both the kids recognised them .... I think so ..... OK ...... The roundabout, got it .... OK I'll leave it on."

Daniel grabbed two forks and put one in each pocket; they wouldn't be much of a weapon but he might be able to do some damage. He went outside, with the intention of collecting his car and driving it as near the restaurant as he could. On the way he deliberately walked close to Barry. Barry looked at him as he passed and for a second Daniel thought he'd made a fatal mistake, as a look of recognition flashed across Barry's face, but then he turned away and walked on. Daniel hurried to his car, very relieved. Behind the restaurant there was a staff parking area. Daniel drove in and parked up.

Barry was in a dilemma. He thought he might just have seen the man in the photograph with the children. He knew he should tell the others. The boss would be really pleased. The trouble is he had seen what Mr McBride had done to his son and then locked him in that cupboard. He was never kind to the children. He couldn't bear the thought of Ben being alone in that place. He had found a phone box some way away and called the police anonymously, telling them where the boy was. He decided to say nothing and prayed that the boss never found out what he had done. He followed Daniel and watched him get in his car and drive behind the Chinese, park up and go into the restaurant. The children had to be in there, he thought. Suddenly he realised George Pamment was next to him.

"Any sign?" asked Pamment.

"No, nothing."

"OK, I'll go and check in the Chinese."

"No need," said Barry quickly, "I've already looked, no sign of them. It was a pretty fucked up photo, I reckon it wasn't them at all. I said we shouldn't have told the boss until we'd checked it out. He'll be bloody furious when we get back with nothing."

"We'd better tell him we found the people in the photo and it was someone else completely. We'll tell Jarvis the same thing. What do you think?" said Pamment.

"Yer, probably best, come on, let's find Jarvis and get back to London."

"Also, lets hint at this being all Jarvis' gig and that we were always sceptical. I get the feeling the boss doesn't like Jarvis very much and I reckon he'll be looking for a scapegoat soon; let's give him Jarvis."

Barry thought for a second, "Yair, all right, I can live with that."

Daniel went into the toilets and could hear Ben crying and Lucy trying to console him.

"Don't worry kids, we're going to be fine. Just hang in there for a few more minutes. Lucy, try and get Ben to stop crying, I don't want anybody coming in and hearing him."

He left, paid the bill and went back to their table. About five minutes later a family of five got up to leave. Daniel hurried into the toilets and fetched the children. A woman was in there washing her hands, she looked very surprised.

"Hide and Seek," said Daniel and smiled at her. "Come on kids, I've found you, good place to hide though. Well done."

They hurried out.

"Follow these people, keep your heads down and don't look round. When we're outside, follow me."

They went to the back of the restaurant, got in the car and drove out of the car park. When they got to the first roundabout, they had three cars behind them. An unmarked police car was parked up at the side of the road. It pulled out behind the line of cars and followed on. After a few miles, all three following cars had turned off, and disappeared and the police car flashed its lights and left.

Two hours later, Jackie was sitting in Daniel's living room when Daniel came in and flopped into a chair. Jackie handed him a glass of red wine.

"What the hell was going on up there, sounded as if you were breaking the place up."

"Oh, I was doing an Eli the elephant story; it was a bit raucous, but I had to get Ben to stop thinking about what happened. His fear sort of melted away after a while. I have to say, Lucy is brilliant with him; absolutely ruthless and never stops insulting him, but Ben loves it and totally trusts her. She really handled the whole thing well. Anyway, they're both quiet now, they'll be fast asleep pretty soon."

They both sat quietly for a minute sipping their drinks.

"How the hell did they know we were there?" said Daniel.

"I don't know, it's a long shot, but the only thing I can think of is that they had sent photos of the kids to other gangs, or just cinemas. Maybe they offered a reward if anyone saw them and reported it. The timing would work. If someone rang them when you entered the cinema, it would take them about two and a half hours to get down here."

"Sounds unlikely," said Daniel, "but I can't think of anything else."

"Well, we got lucky but maybe no more trips to the cinema. Do you think I should try to place Ben and Lucy somewhere else?"

"Definitely not," replied Daniel, "they feel safe here, I don't think disrupting their lives again would help at all."

"Says the man who hates kids. To be honest though, that's what I was hoping you'd say."

There was a comfortable silence as they both thought about that.

"When my Robbie was in your maths class, I remember him coming home and telling me you were ripping up the Christmas cards, the pupils had given you. I didn't believe him at the time but then one of his friend's mums told me the same thing. I know you're a mean sod but even for you, that was bit beyond the pale. I always meant to ask you, what was that all about?"

Daniel poured them both some more wine while he tried to remember, it seemed unlikely. Then, in a flash, it came to him, he laughed.

"Ah, I know what you're talking about. That was funny. Do you remember a teacher called Brett Hodges, good looking PE teacher, dead popular with the kids and hated by all the staff, particularly those that taught real subjects and had to mark homework? I still can't believe PE teachers were paid the same as the rest of us. Same goes for art teachers, home economics ..."

"Yes, OK, I get the gist. I'm guessing he was a good mate of yours."

"Absolutely, lovely bloke. Anyway, one year, I bet him ten quid I'd get more Christmas cards than him.

Absolutely stupid really, I had no chance of winning. Anyway, the year seven creep, Walter Watson, known as Winker in the classroom and Wanker in the staff room, always used to be first to give his cards out. Every member of staff got one, even those who didn't teach him.

"So, all the pupils were working quietly in my maths lesson when out comes Watson and gives me a card; it was mid-November for goodness' sake. He also made a lot of fuss doing it to make sure everybody was watching him. So, I thanked him profusely and then, without opening it, I tore it up and threw it in the bin. Don't ask me why, it wasn't planned, it just sort of happened. Anyway, a gasp of shock went round the room and that got me thinking. So, the next card I was given, 'thank you so much, so kind,' rip, in the bin. You can imagine how word got round; I got cards from kids I had never even heard of, let alone taught, just so they could see if it was really true. Every single one went in the bin. I beat hodges by about two hundred.

"Do you know what I remember most? The look of shock on Winker Watson's face and the tear that ran down his cheek. It was the only time I ever felt sorry for him. Not very sorry though."

Jackie was astounded. "I don't believe it; you really were an absolute bastard."

"Yes I know. Still am, I suppose. Doing drama at college is to blame, I guess; I always want to show off, be seen and admired. I also blame my ancient ancestors, all killers and tough guys. My great, great grandfather was Ten Gun Tony of the wild west, you know! Killed dozens of people before they strung him up. Anyway, little Miss Turncoat, what happened to you telling me I was a great teacher?"

"Ten brain cells Tony, more like."

"You know telling you these stories and listening to you tell yours, helps, it calms me down, takes away some of the fear, a sort of normality really."

"Heavens," said Jackie laughing, "you call what you used to do normal; I don't think so."

"Maybe it gives me an inkling of your world. Are you frightened or nervous when you go to work?"

"Every single day," said Jackie, "I've got to go. Look, the most important thing is that they obviously don't know your car or where you live. Just be careful. Good night."

"Don't worry, I will. See you Jackie."

She gave him a kiss on the cheek and left.

Chapter 20 The Assassin

The first time McBride had killed a man was Mr Chase's enforcer. After that, he injured, tortured and beat up many men and women but it was another five years before he killed again.

McBride worked for Mr Chase for many years. Over that time, he gained a reputation for being utterly ruthless. His big break came when he was approached by the gang's solicitor, Peter Richardson, who asked him if he would do a private job, not sanctioned by Mr Chase. It was to get rid of his wife. He offered ten thousand pounds. McBride said he wouldn't do it for less than twenty five thousand. For that, he guaranteed the investigators would not even have Richardson down as a suspect.

When the job was done, the police assumed she had run off with her secret lover, taking her favourite clothes and jewellery with her. She had also, emptied the safe before leaving. The solicitor was able to claim twenty two thousand pounds on insurance. Neither the wife nor her fantasy lover were ever seen again.

He did a few more similar jobs and it made him realise he was getting bored working for someone else. His reputation began to build, and eventually he decided to go freelance and work for anyone who was willing to pay for his services. However, he concentrated on the 'killing for money' side of his business, it was definitely what he enjoyed most.

He told Mr Chase that he was leaving and thanked him for employing him. He insisted he respected him and would never harm him or his business.

A year later, Mr Chase was being driven to a party with his wife but they never arrived. Despite a major investigation, the car and it's three occupants were never seen again. A month later, Justin McBride took over Chase's entire operation.

Pamment, Jarvis and Barry Payne stood in front of Mr McBride's table. They were looking nervous.

"Jarvis," said McBride, "Pamment has given me his version of yet another cockup leading nowhere. What's your take on it."

"Well boss, we had a photo faxed to us that looked promising but when we went down there, there was no sign of them."

"You mean you were too late?"

"No boss, I don't think so. Looking at the picture again we didn't think it was them; to be honest when we were looking round the place, there were loads of kids and lots of them looked like the ones in the picture."

"Show me." Said McBride

Pamment gave him the picture. The problem was, it was a little out of focus and had been handled so often, it was really difficult to see clearly the people in it. McBride studied it and finally put it on the table.

"Well, I can't tell, and I'm their fucking father. So, a wasted trip, what else you got? ..... nothing then.

"Pamment tells me that he and Payne found the people in the photo; they were just locals, but you wouldn't accept that. So, it sounds to me that this was purely your cockup and, in reality, you've contributed absolutely nothing towards the search. In fact, he says you've been more of a hindrance than a help. What have you got to say about that?"

Jarvis looked genuinely shocked. "That isn't true, Mr McBride, I've done my best and we all agreed we should go west with that photo. Pamment never told me they'd found the family in the photo; he's trying to stitch me up, it was Pamment insisted there was a good chance it was them."

"Well, one of you's fucking lying. Barry, I trust you to tell me the truth. Which one of these slugs is lying?"

"Jarvis boss," said Barry without hesitation.

McBride stood up, "Take hold of his arms."

Pamment and Barry took hold of the quivering Jarvis and held him still. McBride walked round the table so he was standing right in front of Jarvis. Jarvis was terrified and a horrible smell started to foul the atmosphere in the room. Without any warning McBride punched him in the face six times using short arm jabs.

"Jesus, he's poohed his pants! Lay him on the floor and put a towel under his arse, I don't want my carpet stained, well, not any more than it already is anyway."

Jarvis was hardly conscious as McBride started a frenzied attack on him, stamping on his face, over and over again. When Barry couldn't stand it any longer, he put his hand on McBride's shoulder.

"He's dead boss, you can stop now."

McBride shook his hand off angrily and glared at both men.

"Get this mess cleared up, I'll be back later. And find those fucking kids."

Still scowling, he marched out of the room. He knew he had to calm down, his frustration was too much, he'd end up killing someone in the street. He drove himself to Blackheath and walked round the heath for an hour, breathing deeply. Finally, he felt able to return to the real world.

That evening he was watching TV, not really concentrating on what was on, but trying to think of some way to find his brats. He didn't really want them around but it was the idea that he was being outsmarted by the police, by social services and despite all his contacts he was not getting anywhere. After a while he realised he was watching a crime drama about a bent lawyer. He chuckled, 'plenty of those about,' he said out loud.

A thought entered his brain and quite suddenly he had the answer. 'God, how did it take me this long,' instead of always fighting the law, he would use it. He would get his kids back through the courts. He picked up the phone and rang his lawyer.

A woman answered, possibly his wife; he had never met or talked to her before.

"Put Roger on." ordered McBride.

"I'm sorry, we're hosting a dinner party. Could you ring him tomorrow at his office?"

"Tell him it's McBride and he's got thirty seconds to get to the fucking phone."

Roger Pettifer reached the phone in what he hoped was well within the time.

"Mr McBride, thank you for ringing, how can I help you?"

McBride went over the details of how Eddie and Zeta had been taken.

"It sounds to me," said Pettifer, "as if the police and social services both acted unlawfully. You've never faced any charges for abusing your children or domestic violence, have you?"

"I think you'd know if I had."

"Of course. I'm not an expert in this area of the law though. I'll talk to some people first thing in the morning and get the ball rolling. I'll be in touch."

McBride finished the call with his stress level having reduced considerably.

Chapter 21 Temptation

The remainder of the winter term came and went. Ben occasionally came home and mentioned that Lucy had got into trouble for something or other, usually fighting with one of the boys. The school didn't get in touch so he decided not to interfere.

During the Easter holidays, Daniel took them out for trips. Two of Daniel's children, Jason and Tess, came to stay for a few days at different times which the children loved. Apart from that, there were dog walks and trips to Weston Super Mare or Taunton or to the beach at Brean. The horse riding was really popular and Georgina said that Lucy was a natural. Lucy pointed out, that must mean Ben must be unnatural.

What Daniel was very aware of, was that the whole atmosphere had changed considerably. The children had been really relaxed and happy before the cinema incident, they felt safe and their old life was behind them. Seeing McBride's men had made them realise that their father, was still out there, searching for them, and they were always slightly nervous.

Ben admitted to Daniel that he preferred being in the house and garden, at school, or at Charterhouse. He didn't really like going anywhere else, further away. Lucy's attitude had changed too, she used to be continually trying to persuade Daniel to go to different places, for days out, but she had stopped doing that. It seemed to Daniel that a lot of her zip had gone.

On the last day of the holidays, they all took Harry to Charterhouse mid-morning. A local farmer was grazing his sheep and they were spread far and wide. It wasn't a problem, Harry liked to watch them but he never chased them. It always made Ben and Lucy laugh; when he first went in the field he would see them and do what he was born to do, he set. It was as if he had never seen anything like them before in his life. Lucy would always say 'stupid dog' and Daniel rebuked her, saying she had probably scarred the poor pooch for life saying such things.

"Well kids," said Daniel, "Easter's over. Last day of freedom, school tomorrow. Massive sums and spellings for you. Peace and siestas for Harry and me."

"Daniel, what's going to happen to us?" asked Lucy pensively.

"You're being stupid now," said Ben, "we'll stay with Daniel and Harry. Won't we Daniel?"

"Be quiet wombat."

"I'm nothing like a wombat."

"How do you know? You don't even know what a wombat looks like."

"Children, children, calm yourselves. I don't know what's going to happen Lucy. The important thing is you're safe now."

"But we can stay with you, can't we?" said Ben, trying to hold back tears.

"I don't know Ben, don't worry about it now, let's see what Harry is up to. Come on kiddywinkles, last one to catch Harry is a three toed sloth."

Lucy trudged away but Ben didn't follow. He hugged Daniel and sobbed.

"I want to stay with you."

"I know, I know."

Lucy, seeing Ben had not come with her, ran back, grabbed his arm and pulled him away.

"Come on dumbbell." She turned back to Daniel. "If you don't want us, we'll be sent back to dad. Won't we?"

"Lucy….."

Lucy glared at him, turned and ran to catch up with Ben. Daniel was almost in tears himself; he didn't know what to say to them.

Neither Ben nor Lucy brought the subject up again but the whole dynamic of their relationships changed after that. Them running in from school and hugging Daniel and telling him about their day and what they'd done, all that stopped. They spent much more time in their bedrooms; they now had their own rooms, and even Harry didn't get the attention he was used to.

Daniel didn't push things, he felt he couldn't make promises that he might not and probably wouldn't be able to keep. Maybe it was a good thing that they weren't so close to him. The problem was, he missed their love and trust.

Tuesday evenings Lucy stayed on at school for football practice. About sixteen pupils took part regularly, some lived in Shipham but some came from other nearby villages, Axbridge, Rowberrow and Draycott.

Lucy was the only girl and made absolutely sure the boys didn't think she would be any kind of pushover. She was skilful but also ferocious in her tackling. Mr Morris, who ran the practice, was forever telling her off for lacking self-control. Once she had a spat with a boy called Colin; a bit of a cocky lad who didn't think girls should be allowed to play. He had made a comment about her being a sissy girl and shouldn't she be at home knitting or washing up. Lucy waited until Mr Morris wasn't watching and head butted Colin in the face. Blood poured from his nose. In Lucy's old school in London, disputes were settled by fights, it was unheard of for anyone to go and report to a teacher, so Lucy was really surprised when Colin started crying and ran to tell Mr Morris. He came over and asked her what had happened, had she really headbutted Colin. Lucy told him it had been an accident; she had backed into him and that Colin was lying because he didn't like her being there. The other players all said they hadn't seen anything; they were all a little frightened of Lucy. Mr Morris was sure Lucy was lying, but as it was her word against his he just told her to be more careful in future.

After the incident at Charterhouse, Lucy got worse and Mr Morris had to tell her off more and more for being over robust when playing. Several times he had made her sit out for a while to calm down and he had warned her he would stop her coming altogether if she continued being so violent to the others. Lucy hated Mr Morris; like most of the men she had met in her life, she felt he got at her simply because she was a girl, the boys were always getting away with stuff.

One Tuesday, a boy called Tim, had done a clever manoeuvre to get past Lucy with the ball, which left Lucy looking silly, so she thought. She ran after him and slid into his ankle. It was a terrible tackle but luckily Tim wasn't badly hurt. He got up and pushed Lucy to the floor. She leapt to her feet, swearing at Tim, but before she could take revenge, Mr Morris got between them and held Lucy's arms until she had calmed down. He ordered her to leave the pitch and go and sit on the bench at the side. She spat on the ground but did as she was told. She'd find Tim and teach him a lesson at school tomorrow.

A few minutes later Mr Morris blew the final whistle for the end of the practice session.

"That's it everyone, off home now, see you next week. Lucy you stay for a minute."

The boys trudged off to walk home or meet their parents in the car park at the front of the school. Mr Morris sat down next to Lucy and turned to her.

"What did you think you were doing Lucy; you could have broken that boy's ankle?"

"He fouled my friend Cliff."

"That was accidental and he didn't hurt Cliff. I'm sorry Lucy but I've had enough. The truth is I do this because I enjoy it. I love seeing young people having fun and keeping fit but It's not fun anymore and that's because of you; I'm always uptight, worried about you hurting someone and being violent. I'm not going to run any more practices with you there. I am going to come to school tomorrow and talk to Mrs Parkin. I am going to tell her that

I will not allow you to attend any further sessions and she should contact your parents and let them know why.

"I haven't got any parents. Nobody wants me."

"Oh, right, I'm sorry that that's the situation but it makes no difference. I can't risk you coming any more, eventually you're going to seriously injure someone."

"Give me one more chance."

"No, I won't, I gave you one more chance last time and the time before that, I'm just at the end of my tether."

They both sat in a miserable silence for a while. Lucy was desperately trying to think of a way out of this.

"If you promise not to tell Mrs Parkin, I'll ... I'll let you touch me."

"Sorry?"

"I'll let you touch me."

She took hold of his hand, which felt limp, and gently placed it on her inside thigh. She slowly moved it up under her shorts. Mr Morris tensed, he went into a trance like state and shut his eyes. His fingers moved up her warm silky skin, but then, when the tips touched her knickers, the realization of what was happening hit him. He pulled his hand back and leapt to his feet.

"NO. No Lucy," he shouted, "what do you think you're doing? Go home at once, oh my God, I'll talk to Mrs Parkin tomorrow."

"If you tell Mrs Parkin what happened," she said angrily, "I'm going to tell everybody that you put your hand up my shorts and touched me. And tried to pull my knickers down. You'll be arrested and sent to jail." She ran towards the road. "You'd better not tell." she shouted.

Mr Morris sat on the bench and thought about how idiotic he had been. He should have stopped it the second she took his hand. He had been naïve and stupid. The trouble was that when his fingers had caressed her knickers with what lay beyond, his body had reacted and for a second or two he wanted more; it had made him feel excited which in itself was really worrying. Thank God he had stopped it when he did. Had he allowed it to continue there would have been no going back.

He tried to think logically what the best thing for him to do was. He decided that not saying anything could backfire. He would see Mrs Parkin in the morning and tell her the truth as to what had happened, up to a point anyway.

The following morning Daniel returned from the shops, having bought the children's favourite pizzas for tea. He noticed his phone was flashing. He checked it and found two messages, both from the school, asking him to come there as quickly as possible, to speak to Mrs Parkin. It was very urgent. He apologised to Harry for leaving him yet again and hurried to the school; hoping, very much, that both children were OK. It certainly didn't sound good.

He was ushered straight into Mrs Parkin's office and seeing her demeaner, he could see it was trouble.

"Please sit down, Mr Pitt. This morning, we had to call a pupil's parents and ask them to collect their child, a boy called Tim, as he had been in a fight and had a facial injury from a punch; he was feeling groggy. I suggested they should take him to the doctors or maybe the emergency department at Weston General, just to be on the safe side. He had been attacked by Lucy.

The parents are understandably furious and want something done. This is the third violent incident in two weeks where Lucy has hurt another pupil. Word is getting round and I am being asked why nothing is being done about it; why am I allowing her to continue attending.

It is a really difficult situation for me. I know Lucy is a special case but, of course, I am not allowed to point that out to people."

"Was she protecting Ben?"

"You're joking, nobody in their right mind would dare bully Ben. It would be equivalent of a suicide mission. No, apparently, it was because of an incident that happened at football last evening, although Lucy said it was because he looked at her in a funny way. She felt he was disrespecting her. I'm sorry, Mr Pitt, but either you're going to have to rein her in or I will have to suspend her. All my staff are complaining about her behaviour and I'm now hearing that some parents are threatening to move their children to other schools. It's a close knit community, people talk. We already have a problem with low numbers, I can't afford this. Anyway, yesterday evening an even more serious incident occurred at football practice. Has she said anything to you?"

Daniel's heart sank even lower. "No, she hardly speaks to me at the moment. Oh God, what happened?"

Mrs Parkin continued. "You probably know that some children from other schools come for the practice; Lucy happens to be the only girl. Apparently Lucy did a dangerous tackle on Tim, yes the same boy, coincidence? Anyway, the boy got up and pushed her over. She went mad and really went for him. Fortunately, Mr Morris, who runs the practice, was close at hand and managed to calm her down. He made her sit out the last five minutes.

"Afterwards, when the others had gone home, Mr Morris, he actually lives in Shipham, you probably know him. Anyway, he told Lucy she couldn't come to football again and he was going to see me in the morning to explain to me why he had made that decision. Apparently he has warned her, a number of times in the past, that this would happen.

"Mr Pitt, I'm terribly sorry, this is going to shock and upset you. Lucy told him that if he let her off she would let him touch her. He asked what she meant and she took his hand, put it on her thigh and pushed it up under her shorts. He was really shaken, withdrew his hand and said no, obviously. She then told him that if he came to see me today she would tell me and other people that he had tried to touch her and remove her knickers and that he would go to prison."

"Oh God, and did she?"

"No, but you can imagine he is really upset. He says he will not take any further practices if she is there. He also says if she makes any false allegations, he will go to court. Win or lose, I imagine that kind of publicity you could probably do without.

"I persuaded him to keep it to himself for now, and we would deal with Lucy; we would make sure she didn't attend any more of his practices. I didn't give him details but I said there was a lot more to this than was obvious and we had to be very sensitive. He's a good chap, he will hold off doing anything for now.

"I'm sorry, Daniel, but this is massively serious, we can't go on like this."

Daniel thought for a few seconds, "OK, I need to think about this. Let me speak to Lucy this evening and see if I can talk some sense into her. I'll keep her home tomorrow. Thanks for your patience, Mrs Parkin, I really appreciate it."

Daniel shook hands with her and walked to the door but hesitated before leaving.

"Does it not seem a little strange to you that after Lucy had said he could touch her, he still allowed her to take his hand, put it on her thigh and push it up under her shorts."

"Well, yes, that did occur to me as well. But on the other hand, he was upset, fed up, out of his depth possibly. He has been doing sports with the pupils for many years and there has never been even a rumour of impropriety."

"OK," said Daniel and left with a heavy heart.

Because Ben and Lucy now had their own bedrooms, Ben went to bed earlier than Lucy at around eight o'clock; Lucy was allowed to stay up another hour.

Daniel said goodnight to Ben and then called Lucy, who was in her bedroom, to come downstairs. They sat in the living room, Daniel in an armchair and Lucy opposite him on the settee. Daniel was aware of an atmosphere of mistrust in the room and Lucy would not meet his eye.

"Lucy, I went to see Mrs Parkin today; well actually she asked to see me. She made me aware of what's been going on and how aggressive you've been recently. and particularly what happened with Mr Morris. Do you know I think if this had been any other pupil she would have suspended you and possibly called the police as well. She is being really kind to us."

Lucy made a noise that made it clear she was not over impressed with Mrs Parkin's kindness or anything else really. It upset Daniel that he had lost her. He had to put this right.

"Lucy. You and Ben have come into my life and, despite all the problems, I have loved having you. And I thought you were happy and we were getting along fine. What has gone wrong?"

They sat in silence for a minute. Daniel left her staring into space and went and made himself a cup of coffee and brought it in with a lemon squash for Lucy."

"If that's true, why do you want to get rid of us?" she said.

Daniel could see she was struggling not to cry.

"When have I ever said that?"

"At Charterhouse. You said you couldn't keep us."

At that moment, Harry, who had been asleep by the door, lazily got up, climbed onto the settee, curled up and put his head on Lucy's lap. Despite herself, Lucy smiled and tickled his ear. Daniel also smiled; he certainly couldn't fault Harry's timing.

"OK, you listen to me Lucy, and you Harry, since it's obvious that you're taking Lucy's side. I never said I wanted to get rid of you nor that I couldn't keep you. What I said was that I didn't know what was going to happen and it's true I don't, it's not something that I will be allowed to decide.

"But it did get me thinking. I took you in as a favour for Jackie. I didn't want to, believe me. I could see it really messing with my nice mundane, quiet life. In the end I agreed as it was only supposed to be for a week or two. Several times since then Jackie has asked me if she should find somewhere else for you to go and I have said no. The reason for that is simple, despite the fact that you're both pains in the butt and incredibly annoying, I've come to like, no, not like, love you, love the both of you very much and, more to the point, so has Harry."

He looked over at Lucy and saw that tears were streaming down her face. He wanted to go over and hug her but he had to keep it together, it was vital she understood.

"So, last night I came to a decision. Please look at me Lucy. If they give me the choice of keeping you and Ben permanently, and, that's what you both really want, then I will, without any doubt whatsoever, say yes, I wouldn't even have to think about it. I would keep you and bring you up as my own. But here's the thing Lucy, if it comes to that, and they decide that it is a real possibility, then they are going to check first how well I've been doing so far and when they talk to Mrs Parkin, Mr Morris and members of the community and they unearth all the misbehaviour, the violence, and the stealing, then there is absolutely no way on this earth they will let it happen. They will think I would be a terrible father. You have to understand that, they will place you with someone else or take you into care. Do you understand what that means?"

Lucy nodded.

"So, the truth is, it could very well end up down to you, not me, as to whether you stay here."

Lucy looked down at the floor for several minutes, Daniel remained silent, he knew that what happened next could define the future for all of them. She stood up and walked over to Daniel and sat next to him. He put his arm round her and she snuggled up to him and cried her heart out. When she had run out of tears, she looked at Daniel.

"Do you really love us?"

"I really, really do."

"If we went into care, would they separate me from Ben?"

"Not necessarily, but it's possible."

Lucy sat in silence and finally said, "Tomorrow, I'll talk to Mrs Parkin, I'll say sorry."

"That's good, but she may not be in the mood to be forgiving, so if she lays into you or gives you a punishment, just take it on the chin and don't retaliate. For goodness' sake don't say or do anything to make things worse."

"I won't, I can be really, really nice if I want to be, you know."

Daniel laughed. "I'm sure you can."

She looked at him and that intelligent cheeky smile that made his heart flutter was back.

"From now on I am going to be a lovely, very well behaved girlie, do ballet, talk proper posh and never pick my nose or scratch my bottom."

Daniel looked at her, folded her in his arms and gave her a long, heartfelt hug.

After two weeks, Daniel had heard nothing from the school. Lucy had obviously talked to Ben, who seemed much happier and a lot less stressed. The great thing was, the old Ben and Lucy were back, maybe not fully but not far off, which was wonderful.

He decided to check how well things were going at school. He picked up the telephone and nervously dialled the school's number.

"Oh hello, could I speak to Mrs Parkin please, it's Daniel Pitt ..... Oh, hi there. I haven't spoken to you for a while and I was kind of hoping that's a positive sign ..... Really? ..... Oh, that's bloody wonderful, if you'll excuse the language ..... She did what? ..... Wow! Mrs Parkin, thank you so much for being so understanding, I know you must have come close to losing your patience and getting rid of her ..... Yes, absolutely ..... Great, thanks again, bye."

That evening, Ben and Lucy got home from school and, as usual, gave Daniel a brief hug and then charged over to make a huge fuss of Harry.

"Hi Daniel, what's for tea, I'm starving." said Lucy, and then continued to try and get Harry to stand still for a second so she could tickle his ears.

Eventually Ben lured Harry to follow him into the garden to play. Daniel could hear him trying to get Harry to drop the ball they were playing with; unsuccessfully it would seem. Lucy walked over for a second hug, but Daniel put a hand up to stop her.

"Just a minute young lady, I spoke to Mrs Parkin earlier this afternoon," he said, in a stern voice.

Lucy looked shocked, "I haven't done anything, anything at all, I promise."

Daniel looked grim. "You certainly have Lucy."

He smiled, "you've been a brilliant student and friendly to all the other pupils, even the boys, for two weeks now. Not only that, but Mrs Parkin told me that you wrote a letter to Mr Morris. You said how sorry you were, and that your bad behaviour was because your mum had died recently, and you were really missing her; nice touch that, clever. You also said that if he could bring himself to forgive you and give you one more chance, you would be really, really well behaved. Anyway, what you don't know is that Mr Morris rang Mrs Parkin to say that you could start going to practices again. However, if you step out of line just once more, you're out for good. Why didn't you tell me you'd written to him?"

She looked him in the eye, and, with just a hint of mischief, said.

"Because if he'd said no, I was going to burn his house down. I didn't think you'd want to know that."

They stood and looked at each other and then, both of them, burst out laughing.

Chapter 22 Bad News

When the call came through, Jackie was sitting at her desk, willing the hands on her clock to tell her it was six o-clock and she could go home. She had had a day of paperwork and was fed up to the teeth. She listened to what was said, thanked the caller and replaced the receiver. She sat still for a few minutes and then rang Daniel. After a while, the call went to answer phone.

"Hello Daniel, I expect you're out with the dog. Bad news, I'm afraid. McBride has brought an action against both the police and social services to get his kids back. It's going to be heard in seven weeks, on the twenty third. To be honest I'm amazed he hasn't done this before. I'll talk to you later, bye."

Some weeks later, the children were in bed and Daniel was listening to the BBC news on the radio. One of the lead stories was that the name of the woman, who had been found dead in a wood near Westerham, had now been released by the police. She was Cora O'Brian, a social worker from Lewisham and had gone missing two days before Christmas.

Harry leapt to his feet growling; a sure sign that someone was pulling into their drive. Daniel quickly went to open the door; he didn't want the doorbell waking Ben and Lucy.

Jackie sat down, Daniel thought she looked shaken and made her a cup of tea.

"By the look on your face I assume you've heard," she said, when they had both settled.

"Yes, just now on the news. How did she die?"

"She was found four days ago. She was naked and buried in the ground in a cardboard box. The pathologist says she died from carbon dioxide poisoning, there were no other injuries."

Jackie broke down and began to sob. She could hardly get the words out.

"Oh Daniel, they buried her alive, she was put in that box and buried alive." She put her head in her hands.

Daniel was shocked, "Oh my God, I am so sorry. How did they find her?"

"It was an anonymous tipoff to the Daily Mail. Daniel, he wanted everyone to know, he's sending a message, a warning to anyone who tries to stop him getting them back in court. The man is a monster.

"My friend in the Met, is certain he is directly responsible for at least twenty deaths and God knows how many injuries, not to mention all the torture he's inflicted on people who have crossed him or just missed they're protection payments.

"Daniel, whatever happens I think I have put you in terrible danger, I am so sorry."

"Well," said Daniel, "I guess next time we go out for a drink, it's your round. There is a way out of this I'm sure, I just haven't thought of it yet. But I'll tell you this Jackie, meeting and looking after Ben and Lucy is one of the best things that has ever happened to me, so don't beat yourself up about it."

They sat in silence for a few seconds. Daniel stood and went to the window, staring at nothing.

"The court hearing is a week Wednesday," said Jackie, "I have to pick up Ben and Lucy the day after tomorrow and take them to a hotel in Bristol. A social worker, who's specially trained for this sort of thing, is going to ask them some questions that the judge has requested. There will be no one else involved. It will be videoed and shown in court. It means the children won't have to attend the court case in person."

"Are Ben and Lucy at risk?" asked Daniel, "Do you think he might try to abduct them from the hotel?"

"No, no one will know in advance, the police officer doing the videoing has no idea what the job is and the social worker won't know the location until the last minute. Believe me, they're safe.

Anyway, the truth is Daniel, he doesn't need to. Unless either Ben or Lucy implicate him, which isn't going to happen, we're going to get slaughtered. I doubt I'll have a job at the end of it; we've broken so many rules. I suppose we did our best."

"It wasn't good enough though, was it?"

"No. It wasn't"

Daniel never had a problem in the mornings getting the children up. The fact they liked school helped a lot, but he also had a secret weapon, Harry. He would let Harry into Lucy's room first and he would leap up and down on her a few times to make sure she was thoroughly awake. Then he would growl at her, mock bite her fingers and give her face a good licking, just to ensure it was nice and clean. No time to dally though; he then rushed into Ben's room. Ben, having heard all the commotion next door, was hiding under the covers. Harry soon scratched those off and gave Ben the same love and attention he had given Lucy. All of them agreed it was a great way to start the day, especially Harry.

Today was different however, instead of getting into their school uniform, they were instructed to put their dressing gowns on and come downstairs. Daniel had prepared a cooked breakfast, something that never normally happened on a school day.

"I have news." he said, "We are going on holiday to Scotland. We are going to stay with Jake, Donna and their new baby, Winter. Best of all for Ben, but not Lucy, they live near a place called Fort William and near there is a very big mountain which we will visit and, hang onto your hat Ben, it is called BEN Nevis, not Lucy Nevis, not Harry Nevis or even, disappointingly, not Daniel Nevis but Ben Nevis. What do you think of that?"

"I'm not wearing a hat!" said Ben.

"You dummy." said Lucy, laughing.

"Now, Jake lives a long way away. So, on the way there, we are going to break up the journey, we will stay the night at Tess's house which is about halfway."

"Great, I love Aunty Tess. Yippy. Where does she live?"

"A place called Kendal in Cumbria, it's in the Lake District."

"Why is it called that?" asked Ben.

"Probably cos there's a lake there, you dimwit," said Lucy.

Ben charged at her. After a few seconds mock fighting, Daniel pulled them apart.

"Actually, there are lots of lakes there."

"A holiday! I'm going to tell Harry." Said Ben and then skidded to a halt. "Is Harry allowed to come?"

"What do you think, Lucy?"

"Of course, I bet he'd love to come."

"Well, you better go and tell him. I expect he's asleep on my bed, he usually has his post nap, nap, between naps, about this time."

Ben charged upstairs and Lucy sat down next to Daniel on the sofa.

"We've never been on holiday before we met you; Dad never took us." She was silent for a few seconds. "He wasn't always kind to us."

"Lucy," said Daniel, "are you able to tell me what your dad did to you?"

Lucy moved along the settee, away from him. "I don't really want to."

"Lucy, I would never ask unless it was really important." Lucy looked at the floor. "Your Dad is trying to get you back. It would really help if we could tell the judge what he did to you."

Lucy was sitting quietly and Daniel could see she was crying and obviously distraught.

"OK, don't worry, we'll manage. It'll be OK Lucy, I promise."

He drew Lucy towards him and cuddled her until the sobs stopped. Daniel reflected on how strong Lucy was most of the time; she would stand up to anyone without a second thought and yet at other times she just seemed to be so vulnerable, emotionally broken. She had experienced such terrible things which made her hard and uncompromising, but what she really didn't cope with was kindness, love and talking about her father.

Chapter 23 Lochs and Mountains

Daniel had not done a long car journey with the children since the very first time he had met them and driven them home. He had some ideas as to how to keep them entertained. Both were sitting in the back and he let things be until the bickering became more than he could handle. Then he suggested the first game, I Spy. It went reasonably well. It was Ben's turn next.

"I spy with my little eye, something beginning with," he thought for a few seconds," with S."

"Inside or out," asked Lucy.

"Out."

Daniel sighed, "Sky maybe?"

"How did you know?" asked Ben petulantly.

Lucy answered. "Cos it's the third time you've done the same word, numbskull." she gently slapped him round his ear.

"Oy, Daniel, Lucy punched me in the face. Stop the car and throw her out the window and then run over her and then I'll shit on her body."

"Woah, Ben, stop, that was seriously horrible." said Daniel, genuinely shocked.

"Which bit?" asked Lucy.

"I have no problem with him throwing you out of the car or running over you, which you thoroughly deserve, but the last bit was horrible."

"Sorry Daniel, it sort of slipped out," said Ben, feeling a bit ashamed.

"I know, don't worry, it happens. Hey look, we're now on the motorway. Choose a colour each and count the number of cars that you see of your colour. The one who sees the most before we stop for lunch in Birmingham is the winner. First prize is extra chips, second prize is less chips, third prize, no chips."

"I'm red and I've seen ten already." shouted Ben.

"No, you haven't you little cheater," said Lucy.

"Oh my God," said Daniel, wondering if he was going to survive the journey intact. 'Thank heavens it's only two hundred miles to go!' he thought.

They stopped at a service station about fifty miles past Birmingham, and Daniel reflected that, actually, the journey hadn't been too bad so far. He'd put a cassette tape on of The Hobbit and Lucy had listened avidly and really enjoyed it. Ben had listened for a while and then fallen asleep. Daniel had watched in his mirror as Lucy had put her coat over him to keep him warm. Daniel smiled to himself and wondered again how anyone could be cruel to this beautiful and loving girl. Mind you, he thought, she could be a little wild as well. More than a little in fact.

It was quite cold, but they had to sit outside at the service station. Harry wasn't allowed inside so they had no choice. Daniel went to buy sandwiches, crisps, drinks and some chips and they all tucked in. Harry was only given a single treat and looked more than a little disgruntled.

"Kids, I want you to listen carefully. I am going to drop you off at Uncle Jake's house tomorrow and leave you there for a day or two. I have to fly to London tomorrow night. Now you have to be really well behaved while I'm away; I'm relying on you. Jake and Donna have a new baby and it's a stressful time for them. And you must make sure Harry is fed and looked after. Can you do all that?"

"Yes," said Ben.

"We promise," Lucy added.

Daniel said, "Ok, thanks, that's great, I have some really good news though. I can tell you there have been some developments and, you will not be going back to live with your father, it's not going to happen. I've sorted it."

"Are we staying with you and Harry?"

"I'm not sure Ben, I hope so, but whatever you hear from other people or on the TV, trust me, you're not going back to your dad.

"How have you managed that Daniel?" said Lucy.

"It's not important Lucy, but I promise you, it's true. Now, listen carefully, this is very important. Lucy, this envelope is for Uncle Jake but you are not to give it to him tomorrow. You must give it to him on Thursday afternoon, round about four. Do you understand, Thursday afternoon at four. I've written it on the back of the envelope. And don't forget, Jake and Donna have a new ...."

Lucy interrupted him, "Ya, ya we know. Don't go on."

Ben giggled and in the end Daniel couldn't help but laugh.

"You cheeky monkey. Come on let's take Harry to the field over there and give him a run. On the way, pop the envelope in your bag Lucy, here are the keys to the car."

Daniel and Lucy walked off with Harry. Ben stuffed the remaining crisps and sandwiches into his pockets and ran after them. After all this time, he still felt the need to hoard food, just in case.

That evening, at Tess's house, they were recovering in the living room after a fantastic meal. Tess was a vegetarian and had cooked a nut roast for dinner. Ben and Lucy had never seen or tasted anything like it and Ben had to be coaxed into trying it. However, after one mouthful they were hooked and both ended up having seconds.

"I'm going to be a vegetarian when I'm older and I escape from Daniel," said Lucy.

"Once you're forty five, you can do what you like," replied Daniel.

"Tess, would you mind teaching Daniel to cook," said Lucy, "we get baked beans on burnt toast every meal."

"Last time I only got three beans," said Ben, while rubbing his tummy. He pretended to cry.

"Is that why you've got bread, crisps and chips hanging out of your pocket?" asked Tess, grinning.

"That's the most outrageous lie I have ever heard." replied Daniel while choking on his apple crumble and custard. "I cook beautiful meals for you. If we were a restaurant we would be Michelin four stars. Just for that, I'm cutting your pocket money by half."

"I didn't know I got any pocket money," said Ben, looking bemused.

"Neither did I, what's half of nothing Tess?" asked Lucy.

"Not a lot," said Tess, laughing.

Ben and Daniel went off to the garage where Tess had set up a table football game she had borrowed. Tess and Lucy chatted for a few minutes, then Tess turned the TV on and sat next to Lucy to watch. Daniel did not have a TV, so Tess thought it would be a bit of a treat for her. A minute or two later, she realised Lucy was crying. She turned the TV off and asked Lucy what was wrong, she was worried she may have said something that had upset her.

"I don't really know, I just have this feeling, inside me, that something is going to happen, something horrible. My dad is trying to get us back. You and Daniel are so nice; your whole family is. I've been really naughty and horrible to Daniel at times, but all he does is talk to me and explain what I've done wrong; he never shouts at me, punishes me or even gets angry."

"He was like that with all of us as well," said Tess, "especially after mum died. The truth is, he's a really nice man."

She had to look away and hide the tears welling up in her own eyes.

"You were very lucky to have him as your dad. Was your mummy nice?"

"I think so," said Tess, "it sounds awful but I don't really remember a great deal about her."

"How old were you when she died?" asked Lucy.

"A little younger than you are now. I was seven and the boys were a bit older. She died of cancer. It was quite quick; she was diagnosed and within two months she was dead. I was in a terrible state, I clung to dad for weeks, I didn't see my friends or even go to school, I was wrecked, totally."

"What happened, what did Daniel do?"

"He didn't do anything, he let me cling to him. We just cried together. He told his school he was going to be away for a month and was just there, for all of us, twenty four hours a day.

"The boys acted differently. Jake was twelve, he didn't appear to be affected, just carried on as normal. I'm sure he was devastated as much as I was, but everyone has different ways of dealing with it.

"What about Jason?"

"Jason was ten and went off the rails completely, he got into fights, was badly behaved in school. Dad was just the same with him as he was with you, he never got cross. Of course, he told him to try to behave better but basically just supported him as best he could. I remember one time, Jason swore at a teacher and was suspended. Dad read the letter Jason had been given to bring home. The following morning, I overheard Dad on the phone to the school, he was so angry. He told the head teacher he was a disgrace to the teaching profession, he should be supporting Jason, not punishing him for losing his mum. It was one of only two times I ever heard dad shout."

They sat in silence for a while, both deep in their own thoughts.

"Daniel told us that we were not going back to dad but I don't know if he's telling the truth. I don't want to go back, I really, really want to stay with Daniel."

She started crying quietly. Tess took her in her arms and held her tight.

"I think you should have faith, if my dad says you're not going back to him, then you're not, I've never known him to lie.

"Lucy, if you would like to tell me about the things that happened to you before, you can. If you think it would help. If you don't want to, that's fine as well."

Lucy stopped crying and went limp in Tess's arms.

"If I told you, you'd hate me."

"No, No I wouldn't. I know what it is to feel totally lost. I can't begin to imagine what you and Ben have been through. But know this, I love you, the whole family loves you and Ben and that's not going to change, whatever you tell me."

They sat in silence until Lucy took Tess's hand and squeezed it.

"I want to tell you but you have to promise me that you won't tell anyone else, not even Daniel. You have to promise."

"I promise Lucy, I will not tell anyone unless you say it's OK."

Lucy sat without moving, summoning up all her courage.

"I think my dad killed my mum. He got his men to do it. When I came home from school she wasn't about; that wasn't really unusual, sometimes she got drunk and locked herself in her bedroom to sleep. The following morning, Uncle Barry came to find me and hugged me and then whispered 'sorry'. He was crying. He walked away but at that moment I knew she was dead and I knew my father had killed her."

Lucy began sobbing again and looked at the floor. Tess was totally shocked by Lucy's revelation; she had not expected that. She held her tight and waited, she could tell there was more.

"Dad was horrible to her, he was always shouting at her and hitting her. She drank a lot." She sat still for a minute without speaking. Tess waited patiently.

"He did things to me as well. He would come into my bedroom at night and undress in front of me, he then pulled up my night shirt and touched me. He tried to put it in me once but I was too small. Do you understand what I mean?"

"Yes," said Tess, bursting with despair and an anger she had not known she was capable of feeling.

"He made me do things to him with my hand, sometimes with my mouth, it was horrible. Once he brought someone else and I had to do it to them. At first I said no, but dad sent him out the room and then he punched me." She was finding it difficult to talk as she was sobbing uncontrollably. "I had to do it. I didn't want to."

Tess was also crying, she managed to reply despite her shock and the stupid notion she could make it better.

"Oh, my poor love, my poor love."

She wanted to say more but could not find the words.

They both sat there in abject misery and then suddenly Lucy stopped and stood up, it was like she had flicked a switch and brought a veil down on her feelings.

"I'm going to play football with Ben." She stopped at the door. "When was the other time?"

"What other time?"

"When Daniel shouted."

"Oh, I was playing football for the school team and a parent from the other team was shouting his mouth off, yelling abuse at the referee and some of our players for cheating. Dad was on the other side of the pitch and suddenly yelled out. I remember it clearly. 'Hey twat face, I'm going to give you a choice, either I come round there and punch you in that big fat mouth of yours or you can shut up.' It was really loud and everyone around the pitch watching went silent and the game stopped, all the children playing were looking at dad. Then, suddenly, all the parents watching, started cheering, even the parents from the other team. I couldn't believe what I'd just heard. I was so proud of him, I wanted to run to him and hug him, but it would have been a bit sissy. It was the talk of the school for weeks. He became a hero for a while, and I got to be one of the 'in crowd' because of that."

"What did the other bloke do when your dad yelled at him?"

"He shut up." She looked thoughtful. "I think he made the right decision; Dad isn't really one for empty threats and he's pretty strong."

Lucy walked to the door and turned. "One day I am going to kill him, my dad. I'm going to make him suffer and then kill him." She walked out.

Tess sat thinking about what she had just heard, she had no doubt Lucy meant it. She tried to imagine what it must be like to live in that toxic environment, and to know that the one good person in your life had been murdered by the person who should be loving and protecting you. Tess prayed that one day Lucy would be able to refer to Daniel with the words 'our dad', instead of 'your dad'.

The following morning, they left early and, as Lucy was giving Tess the longest hug she'd ever had, followed by a kiss goodbye, she whispered, 'I love you, and, thanks for listening.'

"I love you too Lucy, I will always be there for you."

Lucy looked at her with tears in her eyes, she couldn't think of anything else to say, so she waved and got in the car.

They arrived at Jake and Donna's house at lunch time, having done the journey without a break. They got out of the car and stretched. Jake came out of the house to greet them, followed by Donna, who had the baby in her arms. They all hugged each other. Lucy asked if she could hold the baby. Donna was a bit nervous but carefully gave it to her. Jake opened the boot to let Harry out, who charged around exploring every part of the front garden. Jake then grabbed their bags and they went indoors.

"Can I carry one of the bags?" asked Ben.

"Ok," said Jake, "it's quite heavy though."

"You're too weedy and squirty to carry that bag," said Lucy.

"I am not, tell her Daniel and I'll give her a bunch of fives."

"Enough," said Daniel, "Ben, you may take the small bag. Lucy, behave, stop trying to wind your brother up. Don't worry Donna, they only bicker twenty three hours a day; you always get an hour off."

Jake watched Ben trying to carry the bag,

"That's more like dragging than carrying, here let's do it together."

Donna took Lucy, Ben and Harry to show them the back garden. At first she had been concerned about Lucy carrying the baby, but she could see how careful Lucy was being and stopped worrying. Daniel and Jake settled down in the sitting room.

"What's happening with the children?" asked Jake.

"Well, they were interviewed last Friday by a social worker. The judge turned up to watch apparently. It seems they didn't say anything that implicated their father."

"So, what happens now?"

"I think they will be returned to him. Hopefully, the judge will insist on regular checks on them."

"Oh, sorry Dad, that's a real bummer, but I'm not quite sure why you're here, not that it isn't good to see you."

"Actually, I want to ask you a favour. I wanted them away from the press and publicity, that's why I brought them here. Would you have them for a few days? Tomorrow, I'll leave the car here, fly back for the verdict, then when I get back, I can explain to the kids what's going to happen to them. I'll drive them to wherever the court has specified as the handover point."

"It's awful, poor little things."

"Are you OK having them, do you think Donna will mind?"

"I'll check with her but I'm sure she won't. I'll take a few days off; we'll take them to the beach and stuff. I'm glad you brought Harry; he'll keep them busy."

"Watching them all in the garden, I think your problem will be separating Lucy and Winter. They look so happy together.

"Ok, well look, the verdict is tomorrow afternoon and if it goes against us, the judge will give instructions as to what happens next, so, I've got a flight booked in the morning to London and another booked on Friday, back to Inverness. I'll get a taxi back here. Then I'll drive the kids to wherever the judge has ordered. Thanks so much for doing this. In the meanwhile, I'd like to show them Ben Nevis this afternoon, fancy coming?"

"Great, we'll have to go in your car though, Donna's got a baby clinic appointment."

"Nothing wrong is there?"

"No, just a checkup."

Later that afternoon, they parked in a small parking area at the side of the road and walked to a narrow footbridge crossing a fast flowing stream. It was a beautiful scene, purple heather interspersed with small yellow flowers in the fields around them. Cows and sheep were calmly munching grass and the only noise was the gurgling of the stream below and an occasional car, half a mile away on the road.

"Wow," said Lucy, "I thought the Mendip Hills were pretty cool but this is amazing."

"Look, that's a big hill," said Ben staring in awe and pointing at the mountain dominating the view in front of them.

"Well Ben, that is Ben Nevis," said Jake. "It's the tallest mountain in the whole of the United Kingdom, that includes England, Scotland, Wales and Northern Ireland.

"Have you ever been to the top?" asked Ben.

"I have, many times, you can walk and scramble up but you can also choose other routes where you have to do some quite tricky climbing. I've done both, I love that sort of thing. You have to be very careful though, properly kitted out and prepared. It's supposed to be the second most dangerous mountain in the world. The weather at the top the mountain is often not the same as at the bottom and sometimes can change rapidly. On average three people die up there every year.

"Now, if you look over there, do you see the old ruin, no I don't mean Dad. That's Old Inverlochy Castle."

"It's all broken up," said Ben, obviously not very impressed.

"Oh, well maybe it is Dad then. No, actually, it's in good nick considering it was built eight hundred years ago. Goodness it really does sound like Dad now."

"Alright, enough with the funnies," said Daniel, "You're already out of the will."

"Sorry Dad. Anyway, a powerful clan or family built it in twelve twenty. It's seen a lot of battles has that castle. Ben, control yourself."

Ben was still giggling at Daniel being called an old ruin.

"Wow!" said Lucy, "This place is just incredible. What's that down there?"

"That's the railway line that the Jacobite express runs on. It goes from Fort William to Mallaig. It's a steam train."

"What does that mean?" asked Ben.

"It's an old fashioned train that runs on steam from burning coal or wood. Smoke comes out of a funnel on the top. We might go on it while you're here. Oh, and that river below us is the River Lochy. It flows along, what's called, The Great Glen, that means valley, from Loch Lochy to Loch Linnhe, near Fort William."

"What does loch mean?" asked Lucy.

"It's the Scots word for lake."

They stayed for another half hour while Ben and Lucy plied Jake with question. Daniel was incredibly proud of them. He didn't think many modern kids would be interested in all this. Finally, they walked back to the car.

"I loved coming here, it was great." said Ben, "I liked Ben Nevis best. I'm going to go to the top one day. Lucy, you see that very small hill over there, that's probably called Lucy Nevis."

Lucy shoved him in the back and he fell on the grass.

"Oh, so sorry Ben, my hand slipped."

Ben leapt up and charged at his sister but before he reached her, Jake grabbed him by the arms and twirled him round and round until he was giddy. They all laughed as

Ben tried to keep his balance as they walked back to the car.

After a late dinner, Ben and Lucy went up to bed. They were sharing a double bed in the spare room. Daniel told them they could have a quarter of an hour reading their books and then he'd come up. Jake and Donna both went up to say their goodnights, Winter didn't accompany them as she was already asleep. When they came down Donna was close to tears.

"It is just so upsetting that this might be the last time we'll see those lovely children. It must be ten times worse for you Daniel. I don't know how you are coping."

"Believe me, it's not easy Donna, I just try to stay positive and not think about all the bad things that could happen. Mind you, when you've had them on your own for a day or two, you might well think differently."

"I don't believe that Dad, when you think what they've gone through, they are incredibly well behaved. They do exactly what you tell them without any argument and I've never known children so interested in nature and stuff, they were amazing at Ben Nevis."

Daniel knew exactly what Jake meant but all the same a feeling of depression descended on him.

When Daniel went up. Ben immediately asked.

"Can we have a story?"

"What's the missing word?" asked Daniel.

"Can we have a LONG story?" said Lucy with a twinkle in her eye.

"Pleeeese," said Ben.

"OK, just a short one then. We'll do the 'Mister men came to say goodnight' story."

"Oh no!" exclaimed Ben and Lucy together.

"We'll start with Mr Bump. And then along came Mr Bump."

The children got out of bed and Daniel walked around regularly bumping into each of them and knocking them onto the bed. Each time he would say whoops, sorry or oh dear. Lucy and Ben would fall in an exaggerated way and make an 'ouch' sound. It was a very noisy game and soon Jake and Donna came to see what was going on.

"Will we wake Winter," asked Daniel, suddenly feeling guilty he'd been so thoughtless.

"No, I don't think you will," said Donna, "she's downstairs in her room and we've shut the door. Solid stone walls. Anyway, she has to get used to noise."

"Well, the next person is Mr Clumsy, he's come to say goodnight," said Daniel.

The children jumped into bed and Mr Clumsy walked around the bed but this time tripped and fell on top of them at regular intervals.

Finally, Mr Tickle arrived. Very quietly and slowly Daniel would sing 'and along comes Mr Tickle' and each time his hand would come closer and closer to a side, leg or foot and then suddenly pounce and tickle mercilessly. The children screamed and tried to escape. After five minutes everybody was exhausted.

"He used to bully Tess, Jason and me with that game when we were little. Wait till he does the typewriter on you." Jake laughed at the memory.

"What's the typewriter?" asked Lucy.

"Let's hope you never find out." replied Jake, "has he taught you his song; daddies handsome?"

Ben and Lucy shook their heads.

"Right well it goes like this." He sang. "Daddies handsome and clever and intelligent and sophisticated and beautiful." We had to sing it with him and if anyone didn't, he'd prod them really hard with his fingers, it was very painful.

"God, that's torture, Daniel," said Donna, feeling quite shocked.

"Don't believe a word of it, Donna, he was always a bit dodgy with the truth." said Daniel. "Anyway, that's it, go to sleep now kids,"

Jake and Donna left, feeling a little worried that putting Ben and Lucy to bed was not that straight forward.

Daniel gave Ben and Lucy an extra-long hug and a kiss.

"I'll be gone when you get up tomorrow, the taxi's picking me up at five o'clock in the morning. Remember, be good, helpful and kind, and Lucy, don't forget to give Jake the letter. See you in a few days."

"Bye," they both shouted.

Daniel went out and shut the door. Halfway down the stairs, he sat down and quietly wept. Harry sidled up and sat next him.

"Bye old friend," said Daniel.

Chapter 24 Endgame

BBC Newscaster

'After a high court hearing that has lasted two days, Judge Norma Thomson has ruled in favour of Mr Justin McBride in a case to establish if his children should be returned into his care. Ms. Thomson pronounced that, although Mr McBride has been in court for violent crimes a number of times in the past, he has never been convicted. The judge ruled there was no evidence to show that Mr McBride had ever abused his children or was anything other than a good, caring father.

Social services had argued that the children would not be safe. Earlier this year it was suspected that the children's mother had been murdered, however, her body had never been found. No arrests have been made and the investigation is ongoing. Mr McBride's solicitor told the BBC that his client believed she had a secret lover and it was most likely that she ran away with him. However Mr McBride did not know his name.

In her summary, Judge Thomson said that despite Mr McBride's fitness to be a parent, the two children should be regularly visited and monitored by a social worker. She ordered the court to convene the following afternoon and she would give her official verdict and arrange how the children should be handed over. She will also give details as to the frequency that the children should be visited by social services. The father of the children, Mr Justin McBride, was not in court today but has been ordered to attend tomorrow.'

The case was high profile and the newspapers had had to tread carefully. McBride's links to organised crime were well known but he had never been convicted and cases against him had always failed, often because key witnesses failed to turn up to testify or just disappeared altogether. However, he had never been accused of mistreating his children.

The following day, the judge gave instructions that the handover must take place within seventy two hours and that whoever was looking after them now, should contact Lewisham police to arrange it.

Outside the court there was a large crowd, including many reporters and tv crews. McBride's solicitor came out first and from the top of the steps leading to the court building he made a short statement on behalf of McBride.

"We would like to thank Judge Thomson, who presided over this case so expertly and came to the right decision.

Mr McBride has been treated appallingly by both the police and social services. They have acted outside the law as if he is some kind of criminal and child abuser. There is not a shred of evidence to support this and he has never been convicted of any crime. In the next few weeks, he will be suing, and demanding compensation from the organisations and individuals who have put him through this terrible ordeal. He is very much looking forward to seeing his beautiful children once more and taking them home where they belong. Thank you."

A few minutes later McBride came out, flanked by Pamment, Fenton and Barry Payne. He waved to the onlookers. He was wearing grey slacks and a bright friendly jumper and was smiling. His bodyguards were quite taken back by this. None of them could ever remember seeing him smile before, nor wear anything but a dark suit.

Daniel had arrived at the court early and was at the front of a group of reporters. He was wearing a long sleeved coat and was carrying a microphone. Watching the group come down the steps, he realised that one of the men flanking McBride was staring at him and had obviously recognised him. His body turned to ice; he knew his plan had failed. But then something extraordinary happened. The bodyguard, Barry Payne, seemed to do a slight shake of the head towards him and then look away and continued down the steps.

As McBride came level with him, Daniel stepped forward and shouted as loudly as he could, above the melee.

"Mr McBride, now you've got your children back will you continue to beat up your six year old son and rape your nine year old daughter?"

McBride stopped dead in his tracks.

"What did you fucking say?" he snarled as he turned to face Daniel. His bodyguards tried to stop him but McBride pushed them out of the way.

"What did you fucking say?" he repeated as he moved towards him.

"I said, will you carry on beating up your six year old son and raping your nine year old daughter?"

The whole area had gone silent, and every camera was pointing at the two of them. McBride was by now a few feet away when Daniel pulled his sleeve up, to which the microphone had been attached. In his hand was a pistol and McBride stopped in his tracks. Daniel shot him once in the stomach, and, for a second, McBride stared at him with a look of shock and disbelief on his face and then crashed to the ground. He was lying on his back, shaking slightly and obviously in great pain. Daniel stepped forward so he was standing over him. He was vaguely aware of the panic around as everyone ran for cover in all directions, save for a few brave journalists who continued to watch or film.

McBride was badly hurt and struggling to breathe. He stared venomously up at Daniel and tried to speak.

"I'll kill you, I'll ki,..."

"No, you won't, you'll not be killing anybody else, ever."

Daniel leaned down and held a photograph to his face.

"I want you to know why you are going to die. Look at it." Then he kicked him in the side and shouted, "LOOK AT IT."

McBride looked, and realisation could be seen on his face.

Daniel fired into McBride's body four more times, hitting has arms and legs. McBride grimaced and gasped in agony.

Daniel spoke slowly. "The pain you are now feeling is for Cora O'Brian and Kim McBride and all the other poor sods you've tortured and killed, you murderous bastard."

His shot him between the eyes. McBride's body shuddered once and then was still."

Daniel heard a voice from behind him.

"Let the gun fall to the floor and put your hands on your head." Daniel looked up; two police officers were standing ten yards away pointing revolvers at him. He stood without moving for a few seconds. Tears came into his eyes and trickled slowly down his cheek; his life was over as he'd known it, he would certainly never see Harry again and in all probability his children would not want to see him. Perhaps he should let them shoot him.

"Let the gun fall to the floor and put your hands on your head. If you don't do it now, I will shoot you." The officer said again quietly and calmly.

Daniel dropped his gun. He looked down at McBride and allowed the photograph to fall. It fluttered down and landed face up on McBride's chest.

It was a picture of a frightened six year old boy; his face bore the marks of a severe beating. But it was his eyes and his expression that said so much. Here was a boy who loved and so wanted to be loved in return. He could not understand why the man he adored most in the world was so cruel to him and could not show him any kindness.

One of the police officers handcuffed Daniel while the other picked up the photograph, stared at it, and placed it carefully into an evidence bag.

Daniel Pitt was led away.

Aftermath

Barry loathed the life he had fallen into, the violence, hate and greed. He had to put a stop to it, it was killing him. Days earlier he had made a plan.

As soon as they saw their boss killed, Pamment, Fenton and Barry left the scene. They walked to the car park and set off back to New Cross. Pamment and Fenton were so busy making plans as to how they could take over the business that they didn't notice the car leave the main route and take a quiet road next to Fordham Park. The car engine spluttered and they came to a halt.

"Ere, what's going on Baz, where are we?" asked Fenton.

"The cars playing up I had to turn into a side street," said Barry, "it's a minor problem, I kept telling Mr McBride we should get it sorted properly. I can fix it for now. Only take me a few minutes."

He got out and walked to the boot. He opened it and took out a pistol fitted with a silencer. He walked to the side of the car with the gun concealed by his side and signalled Fenton to open the window. He then shot both men in the head.

"That's for Kim," he said quietly.

He felt very sad that the bloke who was looking after Ben and Lucy had sacrificed his freedom to kill McBride. Especially as McBride would have been dead an hour later anyway.

He concealed the gun in his coat and walked fifty yards down the road and got into a different car he had left earlier. He then drove to the firm's headquarters in New Cross.

McBride had an inner circle of seven men including Pamment, Fenton and Barry. There were plenty of others employed by the firm; pimps, drug dealers, muscle, but they rarely, if ever, came to the New Cross building. They were given instructions by telephone or courier and their payments were delivered to them. The other four gang members were in McBride's office waiting for Pamment and Fenton. They'd heard on the news that a shooting had taken place at the court, and they guessed that the victim must be McBride. They'd also heard that an arrest had been made but there were no other details. They just couldn't believe that the boss might be dead.

Barry walked into the room.

"What's going on Baz?" said one of them, "Did someone kill McBride?"

"Yes I'm afraid so," he replied.

"Well, where's Pamment and Fenton?"

"They've got some stuff to sort out, you know, making sure all our people know that business carries on as usual. We don't want them thinking they can take liberties. Anyway, Pamment says you're to go home and keep a low profile and meet back here at ten tonight. Then we'll work out what to do. I've got to pay off the workers downstairs and lock the place up."

As soon as they had gone, he opened the safe and took out McBride's parcel and the bundle of money.

McBride had always refused to employ any women but had six men working in the warehouse on the legitimate side of the business. Barry gathered them together and explained that Mr McBride had been killed and their employment had come to an end. He gave each of them five thousand pounds and saw them out of the building.

He then drove into the city and dropped off the packages at the solicitors, Telfer, Lilley and Hebden as instructed by Mr McBride. He had lunch at Jo Lyons Corner House in the Strand, and while there, he wrote a letter giving details of some the murders and serious crimes he had observed and where the police could find the four remaining members of the gang that night. He then drove home.

When he walked in, an emotional George and Agnes were waiting for him. They had heard on the news about McBride being murdered. He told them how he had killed two evil men and how he intended to give himself up and cooperate with the police on all the crimes he had been part of.

"Just in case anything happens to me, everything is written down there. Send it to the police anonymously."

He then gave them the remainder of the money; twenty five thousand pounds.

"Thank you for everything," he said, "You've been wonderful, you've been my mum and dad and given me love for the first time in my life and I'll never forget that."

"Son," said George, who was crying with grief, "I'm so sorry I got you involved with McBride. I never would have done it if I'd known and it seems a weird thing to say to someone who's just killed two people but we are so proud of you, you are our son and we love you. And if we're lucky enough to be alive when you come out of prison, we'll be there at the gate to meet you."

"And if we're not alive," said Agnes, "this house will be yours to live in if you want."

With tears streaming from his eyes, Barry hugged them both and left.

Half an hour later, he walked into Lewisham police station and went up to the counter."

An oldish officer was on duty. "Yes sir, how can I help?"

"I want to report a murder, well actually two murders. And tell you where and when you'll find four violent criminals."

"Oh, really sir, and who committed these murders if I might ask?"

"I did," said Barry and placed the gun on the counter.

Three months after being charged with murder, Daniel Pitt pleaded guilty at The Old Bailey. He was given a life sentence with a minimum of fifteen years in prison.

Jackie was taken before a police tribunal; she was given a written warning and a demotion to sergeant.

McBride was as much a vindictive man in death as he had been in life. A month after his demise, Telfer, Lilley and Hebden, a respected firm of solicitors in London, followed the wishes of their client, Justin McBride. They had been instructed that four weeks after his death they were to open the parcel and inside they would find five smaller packages. Each one had an address on it. All they had to do was stamp and post them. The recipients were – The BBC, The Guardian, The News of the World, The New York Times and finally, The Crown Prosecution Service. In each package were documents and audio tapes proving beyond doubt that nine men, each paid twenty five thousand pounds to McBride for him to murder their – wives, business partners or criminal rivals. Some had paid extra to have their victim tortured first. Also, there was categorical proof of bribes being paid to five very high ranking police officers for protecting McBride from both arrest and prosecution. This included both altering and faking witness statements and other evidence. One of them was an assistant chief constable in the metropolitan police.

All of the men involved were arrested and charged with a variety of crimes including murder for some. Approximately a year after McBride's death, when these started to come to court and the full facts of his crimes came to light, there was an outcry over Daniel Pitt's sentence. Many people including some members of parliament felt that, in the circumstances, it was too harsh. The judiciary disagreed and stated that their hands were tied.

However, six years into Daniel's sentence and after a great deal of pressure, the Lord Chancellor advised the Queen to pardon Daniel and five months later he was freed.

After Daniel was arrested, Ben and Lucy had stayed at Jake and Donna's house for three weeks but both the children were unsettled, particularly Ben, who felt Daniel had abandoned them, he had no concept that Daniel had sacrificed his own life for them to be free of their father for good. Donna, in particular, was not coping with them very well and in the end social services organised for them to be fostered with a young couple called David and Chris Sayer. They lived in South Somerset and could not have children of their own. They had never fostered before, but found, almost immediately, that they enjoyed having Ben and Lucy and formed a bond with them. They had changed dramatically from the two children that Daniel had picked up on the M4, almost a year earlier, and the love, kindness and structure that he had given them had paid dividends. They were willing to give the Sayers a chance and they did not fall short. Within a matter of months, they were a real family but this time without the fear of being torn apart.

As soon as they were allowed, David and Chris adopted Ben and Lucy. At first the children missed Daniel but slowly the realization came that their old life of fear was gone forever. They had a mum and dad who loved them and weren't going to disappear.

One day Chris asked the children if they wanted to revert to their old names but they both said no; they would stay Ben and Lucy.

The police continued to look for Kim, but when Barry gave evidence that he had taken part in the lead up to her murder and was certain she was dead, the case was closed, even though her body was never found.

The Sayers paid for a tree to be planted on Blackheath, near the children's first home. At its base was a stone with an inscription which read.

In loving memory of
Kim McBride
Much loved by her children
Ben & Lucy

Without fail, every year on the anniversary of their mother's disappearance and probable death, the Sayers took the children to see it and encouraged them to allow their emotions to run free and talk about the nice things they remembered about their mum.

Three weeks after the adoption, Ben and Lucy got home from school to find David standing outside beaming.

"I have a surprise for you two, but you have to guess what it is,"

"Chips for tea," said Ben.

"A holiday in Spain," said Lucy.

"Better than both of those, come with me, and you must keep your eyes shut. No peeking Ben."

He carefully led the very excited children round the outside of the house to the back garden, he ushered them through the gate and then stood aside.

"OK, you can look now" said David.

The children opened their eyes, and there, at the end of the garden, stood Chris, desperately hanging on to Harry by his collar. She let go and Ben and Lucy screamed for joy as Harry bounded over and tried to jump up into their arms. David and Chris were laughing and so happy that their plan had caused such a wonderful reaction. It took ten minutes for everyone to calm down.

Lucy gave her new mum and dad a hug.

"That's the best thing ever," she said, crying and laughing simultaneously. How did you get him?"

"Well," said Chris, "It was David's, sorry, your dad's idea, he contacted Jake and asked him if there was any chance of Harry coming to us and he said yes, straight away. Apparently he's doing long hours at the moment and Donna was having problems coping with a new baby, a toddler and Harry. So, it all worked out really well for everyone.

Donna and Jake kept in touch with the children, and sometimes sent them pictures of their brats as Jake liked to call them. They and Jason never forgot Ben and Lucy's birthdays and always sent presents at Christmas. Tess and Lucy stayed very close, and Lucy regularly went to stay with her. They remained friends for life.

Years later, when Daniel was set free, he met the children and their new parents at a café near Chard. Lucy was very pleased to see him and thanked him for what he had done but Ben was quite cold. He did not see either of them again for several years, despite being given an open invitation from David and Chris to visit whenever he wished. He never missed sending presents on birthdays and Christmas, however.

Sadly, he never got to see Harry again as he had died some months before Daniel's release.

Despite the efforts of his family, Daniel was never the same again. His mental health had deteriorated markedly in prison and on release he found it difficult to settle. The truth was, he desperately missed Ben, Lucy and Harry. His old life had gone forever.

When Lucy was eighteen, she applied for and was accepted to study creative writing at Bath Spa University. For the first term she stayed with Daniel and was shocked and upset at the change in him. After that she visited him regularly and could tell that he was really pleased that she did. It was only when she was an adult that she really understood how much of his own life and health he had given, so that she and Ben could be free. It seemed so unfair.

About two months after Daniel was released from prison, he heard a knock on his door. He opened it and a woman he had never seen before was standing there.

"Hello," she said, "I'm Kim McBride, and I've come to thank you from the bottom of my heart for what you did for Zeta and Eddie."

Daniel was truly shocked and tried to persuade her to come in but she refused.

"When you killed Justin, I was still an alcoholic. I didn't want the children back. I wasn't capable of bringing them up. Two years ago, I stopped drinking and managed to track them down. They're with fantastic people and so happy. I didn't want to mess with their lives, so I went back to Liverpool. I don't want them to know I'm still alive. I've had cirrhosis of the liver for four years now and the doctors say I haven't got long. But the thing is, I can die knowing that my children are OK. And that's thanks to you. She kissed him on the cheek and was gone.

Jackie had been taken completely by surprise when Daniel killed McBride. She hadn't had even an inkling of his plan. After two years she was re-instated as an inspector.

When she picked Daniel up on the day of his release, fighting their way through rows of reporters and photographers, the first thing he said to her had been that she should not apologise. She had done the right thing all the way through. Every decision he had made was his alone and no one else was to blame.

They remained friends for the rest of their lives but the guilt of effectively ruining Daniel's life never left her.

When Daniel died at the age of seventy three, he left his house and most of his money to his own children and grandchildren, but he also left ten thousand pounds each to Ben and Lucy. He was buried next to his wife, Mary. On his gravestone there was a simple message:

Daniel Pitt

A kind, compassionate and brave dad and friend
who sacrificed his own life for others
We will always love you
You will always be in our heart
from
Jake Jason Tess Ben Lucy
and Jackie

I would like to thank and dedicate this book to the following people.

My wife, Sue, for her massive support and the hours and hours she has spent putting right the many spelling and grammatical mistakes.
(If you come across any that she missed, the blame is hers and the author takes no responsibility whatsoever).

Pete and Carmel for their advice.

My grandson Dan, formatter in chief

Sue Perkins who helps me in so many ways.

The inspirational women of the Cheddar Writers' Club

My children who are always supportive.
(Some of them have even read one of my books).

Val Naden for creating the silhouette for the back cover.

My beautiful dog, Arthur.
Much of the creative side of my writing is done while he and I are walking on the wonderful Mendip Hills.

Printed in Great Britain
by Amazon

45126145R00126